HOW NOT TO

THIEVE

KASS BARROW

Thank you for choosing my book!

Kass x

COPYRIGHT & CONTENT NOTICE

Content Notice:
Adult language and scenes of a sexual nature.

*** This story is written in British English ***

1 – MACKENZIE

The white-gloved waiter elegantly weaves his way around the milling crowds, ready to sidestep at a moment's notice should someone inadvertently stray into his path. Precariously balanced on the upturned fingertips of his right hand is a tray full of champagne flutes. I analyse the silver salver from various angles as he approaches, treating it like a game of Jenga, trying to work out where the tipping point might be. Three glasses have already been taken from the right-hand side, by my estimation, so I'm going to swipe one from the front left. Our paths intersect by the life-size bronze of a well-endowed stallion—Areion of Greek legend—and I hoist a glass cleanly from the tray without incident. I take my fizz over to the nearest marble plinth to feign interest in whatever this pretentious piece of shit is supposed to be. One man's treasure is another man's junk, or whatever that stupid saying is.

God, I hate social gatherings. I hate all the pointless chatter, the posing, and the fakery of it all. All these pompous, bourgeois prats acting like they exist on a different plane to mere mortals. But sometimes needs must. I'm not here out of choice. I'm on a scouting mission, checking the layout of this Kensington mansion, seeing what sort of security system they have in place, and pinning down the exact location of the piece of art I'm interested in. If everything checks out okay this evening, I'll be making another uninvited visit in the not-too-distant future, but it'll be in the small hours of the night, when no-one else is around.

As devoted patrons of the arts, the Belfours often hold these gala events to showcase the work of their latest protégés. It's supposed to be invitation only, to avoid any scum off the streets popping in for free champers and vol-au-vents. However, for those *not* on the invitation list, if you have the right credentials and a thousand pounds wearing a hole in your back pocket, you may apply for entry at the door on the night. As I understand it, "the right credentials" means you have to be either a CEO or an art critic with column inches to your name, but I figured my stated profession of "art historian" was close enough. I flashed my snazzy website at the doorman, and he seemed happy enough to relieve me of my thousand pounds, especially once I'd slipped him a couple of extra fifties on the side. It's amazing how professional you can make a website appear these days with one of those ready-made templates. Of course, it's just a front. My *real* job description would make the doorman's eyes pop. That doesn't mean I'm averse to taking on the occasional bit of legit work. It comes in handy if ever I need to supply a reference to gain access to one of these poncy establishments.

Anyway, here I am, amid the chattering classes, gazing at the latest excuse for creative art by some newcomer called René. To be honest, the marble plinth it's mounted on is more impressive. It's hard to tell what it is, other than a piece of twisted wire, and yet all those around me are marvelling at it as if Michelangelo himself rose from the grave to foist this ugly excrescence on the world. One of the assembled admirers can apparently see the shape of a pouncing cat in the twisted wire; another claims it's the head of a unicorn; yet another claims it represents the tree of life. The piece is titled *Eye of the Beholder*. What that tells me is that even the artist doesn't know what it's supposed to be.

In my peripheral vision, I'm aware of being scrutinised by the person standing next to me. I twist my head to see it's Carmen Belfour—the lady of the house, and quite a handsome creature for someone in their mid-sixties. She's probably wondering who let me in. She's tall and slender with a particularly long neck, emphasised by her chin-length lilac bob. Hanging down the cleavage of her low-cut dress is a long string of pearls, knotted at the chest. I lift my gaze from her breasts to find a soft smirk on her lips, a twinkle in her eyes, and one brow arched. I hope she isn't giving me the come-on. I prefer my meat to be a tad more on the tender side.

"What about you, my dear? What do you make of it?" she asks.

I feign interest, tilting my head on one side and gazing at it thoughtfully as the eyes of the assembled crowd all focus in on me, awaiting my verdict. "It's crap," I declare.

My response is met by a barrage of gasps, but I relent, knowing I really must play nice if I'm to blend in. "You know, scrap metal. A junkyard scene."

"Oh scrap!" Carmen Belfour presses her hand to her heaving chest, the shock of my comment clearly having ripped all the oxygen from her lungs. "Do you know, for a moment I thought you said it was crap. Isn't that funny? My hearing must be going."

Polite chuckles ensue from the other bystanders and I offer up a lopsided smile as I mutter under my breath, "Silly old trout!"

"Sorry, dear?" she says, lending me her ear. "Didn't quite catch that."

"Stunning work of art," I shout into her ear making her jump.

"Oh yes, isn't it?" she says, before excusing herself as she spots someone she knows.

I meander through the crowds towards the next exhibit.

What I'm really here to see is the Selby collection. Myles Selby is the latest success story to have been supported in his early years by the Belfours. The most recent piece of his to be sold at auction fetched the princely sum of £185,000, but if my intel is correct, one of his paintings here this evening has an estimated value of a quarter of a million. It's called *Maelstrom* and it's a sombre post-apocalyptic scene of London, hauntingly evocative in its grey, beige and black palette.

The Selby exhibit is the most popular, as expected, so it takes me a while to wind my way around the minglers, trying to locate the piece I'm interested in. Eventually I hone in on it. This is the first time I've seen it in the flesh. It's even more breathtaking than I imagined, but it's also...

"It's a bloody print," I blurt out loud.

The person next to me emits a long, languorous sigh. "Yes. Pity, isn't it."

His sultry baritone piques my interest and I

twist my head to see a suave-looking gent in his mid-forties, wearing a silver-grey suit, jacket unbuttoned, hands thrust deep into his trouser pockets. I turn to face him full-on and I'm met by a pair of piercing blue eyes, a lazy smile, and cheekbones to die for. He eyes me up and down hungrily, licking his lips with relish, as if he'd like to slap me between two buns and gobble me up. He reminds me very much of Mads Mikkelsen in the role of Hannibal Lecter. My gaze drops to his mouth and I start to imagine what that lazy smile of his might taste like.

He holds out his hand. "William Fletcher. CEO of Fletcher Holdings."

I grab his hand and give it a firm shake. "Mackenzie Oden. Art Historian. I was rather hoping to see the original."

He shoves his hand back in his pocket and shifts his weight to his right hip—a relaxed stance that gives the impression he's happy to stick around and chat with me awhile.

"I understand it was to have been on display here," he explains, "but it got whisked away at the last moment for another exhibition."

I groan. "Where at?"

"Tate Modern. They're showcasing the rising stars of local talent in a special exhibition called *The New London Set.* Selby's piece got a last-minute invite due to the publicity surrounding his latest sale. If you want to go and view the original, I believe the exhibition is on for the next three months."

"Oh marvellous!" I grouse. "So I've paid a thousand pounds to come here and gawk at a print."

"Well, it's still pretty damn spectacular," William points out, "and the print run is limited to just fifty, so if you're interested you better put your order in. I've already signed up for my copy."

I huff to myself and knock back the glass of champagne. My client isn't interested in a bloody print and neither am I, so it looks like I've had a wasted evening. The Tate Modern is too high profile a target for me to consider and I've no idea where it's going to be housed after it leaves the gallery.

"Even the bloody champagne is warm," I grumble. "Is there a bar here?"

"I'm afraid not but..." he pauses and moves closer so I can feel his warm breath feathering my cheek. "I do have a rather nice bottle of Château Fonbadet at home that I've been saving for a special occasion."

My broad grin gives him all the response he needs.

Looks like it's not going to be a completely wasted evening after all!

2 – AIDEN

I suppose I should be thankful I was born a Foxwell, but these days being a minor member of the aristocracy is as much a burden as it is a privilege. It still comes with certain standards that must be maintained, and yet any kind of profligate lifestyle is frowned upon in this era of austerity and eco-anxiety. People might think my life is all champagne and caviar, but it's actually pretty lonely and depressing being me. I rattle around this big old house with just my dad and the staff for company—mostly just me and the staff, in fact, since my dad is always off doing his own thing.

I like to sneak off and do my own thing too, whenever I can. I say "sneak" because my dad wouldn't approve of where I go. Foxwell Manor, where I live, is in the middle of nowhere so I have to find my entertainment wherever I can. We live in Norfolk, in eastern England, about twenty miles from the coast, in a tiny village with no amenities whatsoever. Six miles away in the next village to the west, there's this gay couple I like to visit. They're called Kelly and Grant and they're like the older brothers I never had. They have an open house policy for the gay community, so it's a good place to go and meet new people, but my dad wouldn't approve because he still clings to the hope of marrying me off to some "respectable young lady from a good family." I'm supposed to keep my true sexuality under wraps until I've supplied him with a grandchild to continue the family line. He tells me that once I've done the deed and produced an heir, he doesn't care what I do after that. That's the carrot he dangles in front of me.

"Do this one thing for me, Aiden, and then you can indulge yourself with as many men as you like on the side and I'll still support you."

By support, he doesn't mean emotionally, he means financially. In other words my dad is blackmailing me. If I publicly come out as gay he'll cut off my allowance and take away all my toys, including my car. He's even hinted that I'll lose my inheritance, but I'm not sure if that threat really holds water. I mean, who else is he going to leave it to?

Anyway, for now I content myself with my secret trips to Kelly and Grant's place. Kelly's another one who's always trying to play matchmaker, except he wants to fix me up with a "nice boy my own age" when he knows perfectly well I prefer older men. Not that I have a lot of experience of relationships on account of me being super fussy. As my dad is keen on pointing out, I live in a fantasy world. The men in real life don't tend to match up to the brooding anti-hero who inhabits my dreams. He's a man-of-mystery who lives an exciting and glamorous life, and probably even has a separate summer and winter residence. Maybe somewhere like Lake Geneva, in Switzerland, for his summer residence, and in winter I picture him up a snowy mountain in St. Moritz, partying on absinthe into the small hours before skiing back to his log cabin. Yes, I've been watching too many spy thrillers and I have my heart set on a tall, dark, handsome stranger—a man who's uber-sophisticated, extremely capable, slightly dangerous and sexy as sin. *That's* my type, but I'm not going to find anyone like that around these parts.

I hate my life. My future is supposedly mapped out for me, continuing to run the family estate, but that doesn't exactly fill me with glee. This isn't even a real home. It feels more like a mausoleum, haunted by a sense of duty to all the previous generations of Foxwells who have lived here. People come and go but the bricks and lime mortar remain, outliving us all. It's like our only real purpose is to service this property, to maintain it and pass it forward to the next generation. I wish I could hire a modern-day Guy Fawkes to plant some gunpowder in the wine cellar. I think I'd be doing the world a favour. We're probably personally responsible for one of those icebergs breaking away from the polar ice shelf. Foxwell Manor is a cold and creaky place and it takes a bucket load of money to heat up, most of which leaks out straight into the atmosphere. It's a listed building so we can't change too much about it. It has open fires in all the reception rooms; high ceilings throughout; leaded windows; tiled floors with no damp course beneath; a great hall with a full-height hammerbeam ceiling; and...well, you get the picture. It's not really a sustainable family residence. At best, it should be a tourist attraction of how the aristocracy *used* to live.

I wish I had the courage to leave this place, but it's an alien world out there to me. I've never had to stand on my own two feet. I have no concept of surviving outside the trappings of wealth and that makes a coward of me. I can't stomach the thought of running away and living on the streets. And I would have to because I have no money in my own name. My dad keeps me here by means of a very short leash with only enough of a cash allowance to meet my immediate needs. But I've reached that age where I'm feeling both restless and reckless. I feel like life owes me a crack at finding out who the *real* Aiden Foxwell is when he's let loose.

3 – MACKENZIE

I spend a lot of time on the road in my line of work, so my ground-floor pied-à-terre here in Islington is all I need for the time being. It's not my forever home; just a bolthole for when I need to keep a low profile or simply when I'm between jobs. It's convenient for me to have a place in London that's just a few stops on the Tube from my fence, Lenny. He's the middleman who connects me with people in need of my particular talent. He finds out exactly what they're after; determines if it's a feasible target; agrees the price; and handles the whole transactional side. All I have to do is obtain the artwork for the client. It's imperative to have a guaranteed buyer lined up. You don't want to be left holding hot property for long.

I'm hoping Lenny has something else lined up for me after the aborted hit the other night. I'm expecting a call from him this morning, but in the meantime I'm making the most of my lazy Sunday morning with nothing more taxing to do than catch up on the cricket scores.

From my kitchen window I glance up at clear blue skies and consider taking my pot of tea outside, but then my phone rings. I pull it out of my pocket to see Lenny's name displayed on screen. I've known him for years but I still don't know his last name. We don't tend to do last names in our profession. He's known simply as Lenny the Loot. I accept the call, but before I have a chance to say anything, Lenny jumps

11

straight in.

"Hey, Mac, what's up, mate?"

Even over the phone I can tell that behind his gravelly Cockney accent Lenny is wearing a grin as wide and filthy as the new Super Sewer.

"Just having a lazy day at home. How about you?"

"You know me, Mac. Always wheeling and dealing."

"Hey listen, I've got a joke for you." I know how Lenny always likes a good laugh. "Why couldn't the art thief decide what to do with his stolen painting?"

"No idea, mate."

"Because he was sitting on the fence."

There's silence for a few seconds before Lenny says, "Nah, mate, don't get it."

"Sitting on the fence. You. You're a bloody fence."

"Oh, you mean the thief was sitting on me," Lenny says, as if the penny's dropped. I sit through another bout of silence with only the background hum of Lenny's brain cogs whirring away until he eventually replies. "Nah, still don't get it,"

I roll my eyes at Lenny, even though he can't see me. "Forget it. Listen, that Belfour job was a right cock-up."

"Yeah, I know mate, don't worry about it. We've got bigger fish to fry."

"Have you got another job lined up for me?"

"I have. If you're interested."

"Have you ever known me *not* to be

interested?"

"But this is different, Mac."

"Different in what way?"

"This is seriously hot stuff, mate. This is nuclear. This is a leave-the-country type of job."

"What the bloody hell are you talking about?"

"You know my Russian friend?"

"The oligarch fellow?"

"Yeah, that's him. Morozko."

"What about him?"

"Well, he's got his heart set on a Raphael this time."

I laugh. "Very funny! A Raphael? Yeah, and I want the moon on a stick."

"He wasn't joking, Mac."

"Do me a favour! I hope you told him where to go. He might as well ask me to pop over to Cairo and steal the bloody Sphinx."

"Normally I would tell him it's a non-starter, but..."

"But what? There's no-one crazy enough to steal something that valuable. And you know I don't steal anything that's in a museum or gallery, so why even suggest it to me?"

"Suppose I told you that my Russian friend has heard whispers about a Raphael being held in a private collection."

"Impossible. None of his are held privately."

"What about the one the Nazis stole during the Second World War?"

"What about it? It was destroyed in a fire just after the war."

"Was it though?" Lenny postulates. "Suppose the Nazis spread that rumour just so no-one came looking for it? According to Morozko's sources, it's actually been hidden all these years in a bank vault owned by the daughter of a Nazi General. She died last year and once her affairs were sorted, the painting was finally released from the vault."

"Released where?"

"Onto the black market. The only place stolen goods *can* go. The descendants of the Nazi General had no legal claim to the painting so they could hardly sell it through an auction house."

"So why didn't Morozko buy it on the black market when it was released?"

"Earlier in the year he'd acquired a valuable piece from the States and, at the time the Raphael was released, he was the subject of an undercover sting operation by the FBI so he had to keep a low profile."

"So it ended up where?"

"Adorning the walls of a minor stately home on the east coast, just a few miles from the royal estate at Sandringham."

I gasp. "You're telling me there's a bloody Raphael in a private residence somewhere in Norfolk?"

"Yes," Lenny states emphatically. "That's exactly what I'm saying."

"It has to be a fake, surely?"

"Maybe. But maybe not. Just imagine for one second that it's the genuine article. Think about how much that Raphael must be worth, Mac."

"I daren't. You're scaring me now, Lenny. I'm starting to think you're serious about this."

"You don't have to give me your answer right away. Sleep on it and let me know in the morning."

"Sleep on it?" I scoff. "I'm not going to get a wink of sleep now you've laid this at my door. You know I don't handle anything this risky. Can't you ask someone else?"

"It needs someone of your calibre to pull this off, Mac."

"Oh please! Flattery will get you nowhere. What about Winston?"

"Can't lie. I knew you'd be a bit reluctant so I asked Winston first."

"And what did he say?"

"Wouldn't touch it, mate. Said it was too high profile. But then, to be fair, he *is* winding down a bit. I reckon he's lost his nerve, mate. Gonna take someone with balls of steel to take on a job like this. Know anyone with big shiny gonads, Mac?"

"Come on, Lenny. This goes against every rule I've ever lived by. You know my motto. Never steal anything that is so loved by the public it's going to get you in the national headlines."

"But that's the beauty of this. Only a handful of people know the painting still exists. The public won't even have heard of it. The current owner acquired it on the black market, so he can't afford to make a big noise when you steal it from him. It's like the perfect retirement gift to end your career on. We can *both* retire off the back of this. Wouldn't you like to go out in style?"

I huff. "I prefer my freedom to being stylish." I pause a moment as the two halves of my brain begin warring with each other; common sense giving way to the beast of avarice, which sits on my shoulder like a taunting vulture, daring me to go out on a limb. "Just out of interest, how much is Morozko offering?"

"You know he always pays the going rate. Ten percent of true market value."

"Yes, I know that, but what I meant is, how much is he valuing it at? How do you put a price on something like that?"

"Don't know, mate. Maybe he just came up with a price that he thought you wouldn't be able to refuse. All I know is he's offering you a cool £10 million to steal it for him, and me £1 million to persuade you to do it."

"Wow! He *is* serious about getting his hands on it." The greedy half of my brain is starting to dominate my thoughts and I need to take a timeout. "Look, Lenny, this is an awful lot to take in. I obviously need some time to think this through."

"Of course, Mac. I knew you wouldn't let me down."

I sigh at Lenny's assumption that I'm going to agree to do it. "No promises, Lenny. I said I'll think about it, that's all. I'll be in touch tomorrow with my decision."

I end the call and it's only then I realise how hard my heart is pounding. I need some fresh air. I open the double doors leading out into my tiny private courtyard. Picking up my tea tray, I step outside, amid the potted begonias, as the midsummer air wafts over me. I have an old-

16

fashioned striped deckchair that I use for such occasions and I set the tea tray down on an upturned wooden crate that serves as my occasional table.

Once I'm settled with my cup of Twinings, my thoughts immediately gravitate back to the phone conversation. I can't believe Raphael's missing masterpiece has resurfaced. It was supposed to have been lost to the world. This is amazing if true, but if I agree to steal it for Morozko I'll be going against all my rules.

Or will I? It's not like it's being held in a museum, and I've no problem with stealing from a private residence. And yet I can't get away from the importance of the piece.

What the hell are you thinking, Mac? I chide myself, knowing I must be crazy for even considering it. *It's a bloody missing masterpiece! You can't take on a job like this. Imagine the sense of public outrage this would cause if ever news got out. You'd be on Interpol's "most wanted" list.*

And yet, it's true what Lenny said. If the current owner acquired it illegally, he can't go shouting from the rooftops when I steal it from him, so would it really hit the headlines if it changed hands again? After all, there are only a handful of people in the underworld that know it even survived the war.

Shit! It's so tempting and yet I'm so close to retirement I don't want to do anything stupid now.

The only reason I haven't retired yet is because I don't fancy rattling around an old country house on my own with nothing to do. But then again, if I did this one big job, I could seriously upgrade my retirement plans. Forget retiring to the country, I could *own* a country! Well, maybe not a country, but my own private island at least, somewhere beyond the reach of the law. I could spend my days fishing and snorkelling, and I might even write my tell-all memoirs. That sounds like a much more fitting retirement plan to me.

The more I think about it, the more enthused I become. Can I really turn my back on this once-in-a-lifetime opportunity? As Lenny says, it feels like the perfect retirement gift.

I need more information.

Less than half an hour after ending the previous call, I'm back on the phone, quizzing Lenny.

"This minor stately home in Norfolk. What's it called?"

"Foxwell Manor."

"Never heard of it. I thought the landed gentry were all paupers these days. Even the royals have had to open up their palaces to tourists."

"This is true, except canny Lord Foxwell married into city money and he's apparently rolling in it."

"The odds are still very much in favour of it being a fake, but I'll need to spend some time examining it in detail before I can verify that."

"So you'll do it?" Lenny asks, sounding like he's about to jump down the phone line and kiss me.

"I'll investigate. That's all I'm committing to at this stage."

"I know you're convinced it's a fake, but even

you have to know for sure, don't you, Mac?"

"I definitely need to know. I'll never hear the last of it if I don't at least check it out for you."

Lenny laughs. "Too right, mate."

"I'm going to need a way into the household that enables me to properly examine the painting. It's going to take more than a quick look. I'll check if they have any staff vacancies. That's probably the easiest way in."

"Staff vacancies?" Lenny guffaws in my ear. "What are you going to do, mate, pose as a butler?"

"Something like that."

"I've got a better idea. The son might be right up your alley. Yeah, literally. Ha-ha!"

"What do you mean?"

"Rumour has it young Foxwell has a bit of a thing for older gentlemen."

"Is that so? Now that *is* interesting. The lord of the manor has a gay son, eh? Well, that might be just the angle I need to wheedle my way in. Thanks, Lenny."

"Anytime, Mac. I'll tell Morozko we're investigating the matter for him."

"You'd better tell him it's going to take a while. I'm first going to have to gain the confidence of the son so I can get an invite to the manor. I'm going to have to do a bit of detective work so I can find out where he hangs out and arrange to bump into him."

"Okay. Good luck, mate. I'll wait to hear from you when you have news."

"Sure. Enjoy the rest of your day, Lenny. Looks like I'm going to be spending the rest of mine researching Foxwell Manor and its occupants."

4 – AIDEN

When you're born with every advantage all it does is shine a spotlight on your own inadequacies if you fail to make something of yourself. I feel like a ghost. When I look in the mirror I don't see *me* reflected back. I see a lost soul—someone who's shallow and worthless. There is a *me* inside there somewhere; he's just never found a way to break free. There are rules that bind him in place—rules that need to be broken—but am I brave enough to go against my dad? Would I be letting down generations of Foxwells if I fail to produce an heir? Am I the last spindly twig on our family tree? Why is there so much weight of responsibility on my shoulders?

I'm totally conflicted. I want to be a good son and make my dad proud, but on the other hand I absolutely believe I have the right to be true to myself. My dad needs to accept that I'm gay and stop trying to coerce me to fake it in public. How can I hope to make my mark on this world if I start off by denying my own identity? I can't please my dad *and* please myself. I'm in an impossible position.

Someone else who's been put in an impossible position by my dad is our head of security, Frankie. You see, Frankie is the person designated to watch over me on a day-to-day basis. Dad tells me I have to accept this because I'm the sole heir to the Foxwell estate so I'm a valuable asset, but I don't like being babysat. I'm not a kid. Although, after what happened to

21

Mum, I suppose I can understand why Dad's slightly paranoid about something bad happening to me. Mum went shopping in Norwich one day and never came back. She was killed in a hit-and-run. A van mounted the pavement and pinned her to a brick wall. She was killed instantly. The police suspected the van was linked to a robbery but the plates were fake and they never did catch who did it. It's been seven years now, so I guess they never will.

I actually get on okay with Frankie and I totally sympathise with the awkward position he's been put in, but that doesn't mean I'm averse to using it to my own advantage. Dad expects Frankie to keep a vigilant eye on me at all times. I expect Frankie to stay out of my way unless I summon him. Basically he can't win. He's a Foxwell employee. He's *not* my dad. He has no leverage over me, not even if my dad tries to give him such powers by proxy. Dad should wake up and realise that all he's achieving with these arrangements is to alienate and antagonise me. There's a mounting tide of resentment growing inside me and maybe, one day, my rebellious streak will get the better of me. Then who knows what might happen.

5 – MACKENZIE

I've discovered some interesting facts during my online research into my next intended target. I'm a great believer in "knowledge is power." The more background knowledge you have on an intended target, the more chance you have of predicting how they might react in any given situation. I started off delving into the history of the manor house and how a Foxwell came to be lord of the manor in the first place, and then I had a rummage through the gossip columns to see what dirt I could dig up on the current owners.

The peerage and the manor house were bestowed upon the Foxwells during the Elizabethan era, when Thomas Foxwell earned them for services to the Crown. Local government officials wielded real power in those days and Thomas Foxwell rose through the ranks to become Lord-Lieutenant of Norfolk. When the Spanish Armada threatened to invade the south coast, he was responsible for commandeering local merchant ships for use by the British navy, and in so doing he earned the eternal gratitude of his sovereign.

In its heyday, Foxwell Manor was at the centre of a large sheep-farming community. The Norfolk Horn—a black-faced sheep prized for its thick wool and tasty meat—once thrived on the lowlands of East Anglia. Following the decline of the wool industry, meat production became the main source of income for the farmers, but the

Norfolk Horn was not a prolific breeder. Increased demand for meat from wealthy urbanites saw other breeds grow in prominence for their ability to produce a steady supply of fast-maturing lambs. The Norfolk Horn was no longer viable and the Foxwells' tenant farmers began to move away from the area.

All that remains of Foxwell village today is a handful of windswept cottages occupied by hardy folk who have little use for local amenities, and no use whatsoever for a lord of the manor.

Aside from one family member being awarded a Fellowship of the Royal Society, the Foxwells had pretty much fallen into obscurity—as well as financial difficulty—until the current Lord Foxwell married into a family of wealthy city bankers. The Foxwells are now, once again, respected members of the country set, holding regular shooting weekends and charity events on their estate.

These are the dry facts I've managed to garner from my initial research. However, the most pertinent piece of information I came across was in regard to the upcoming charity auction to raise funds for the County Heritage Trust. This annual event always takes place on the second Saturday in August, which means the next one is less than three weeks away. Digging deeper, I was able to uncover some useful information that I can certainly turn to my advantage.

Lord Foxwell's current marital status is widower and he has but a single heir—a twenty-two-year-old son who is a bit of a tearaway, by all accounts. Despite the rumours that Aiden Somerton Foxwell is gay, every year his father tries to fix him up with a bride. A dinner date with the heir to the family fortune is included as one of the prizes for the charity event and, probably to appease his father, Aiden goes along with the farce. The dinner date is always held in the manor house itself, no doubt so Lord Foxwell can ensure Aiden gives a good account of himself. He wouldn't want Aiden running off to a club in London with his lady friend, only to find the photographs of their drunken exploits splashed all over the tabloids the next morning. Lord Foxwell is, after all, responsible for protecting the family's reputation for future generations.

According to the local rag, mothers of eligible young ladies from all the surrounding counties are lining up to pair their daughters off to the heir to Foxwell Manor. But I've checked the small print and there's nowhere in the auction prospectus that says only women can bid. I think the Foxwells may be in for a bit of a surprise this year. It's the perfect way in for me.

I'll ensure I'm the highest bidder, win myself a dinner date with young Foxwell, and then charm the pants off him. It'll be a doddle. I can charm the pants off anyone—man or woman—and I frequently do. This twenty-two-year-old kid is going to be putty in my hands. I'll soon be a frequent visitor, giving me full access to the manor, meaning I can study their security set-up and the painting itself.

You have to be prepared to do whatever it takes to get the job done, but some "duties" are more pleasurable than others. If I have to show young Foxwell a good time to get my foot in the door, then so be it. I won't be complaining, not if the online photos of him are anything to go by.

Sometimes you have to prey on people's emotions to gain access to the premises. That's just the way it is. If that makes me sound like a cold, calculating, callous bastard, that's because I am and I make no apology for it. Sentiment is for losers.

It's the day of our annual charity auction in aid of the County Heritage Trust. I hate my dad for putting me through this every year. Not that I have anything against holding a charity auction, I just don't want to be one of the lots on offer. It feels like my dad is trying to auction off my hand in marriage, rather than just a dinner date, and I know that's how he secretly hopes it will end. I play along because I have little choice. Last time I tried to refuse he took my phone away and locked me in my room until I chilled and relented. This annual event is his baby, that's why he's so hands-on with running the auction when normally he'd delegate it to someone else. He set up this charity event to enhance the prestige of the Foxwell name, so he wants to ensure everything runs smoothly. The family reputation is of paramount importance to him. It's all he really cares about.

The auction is held in the old stable block, which was converted a few years back into an open-plan venue for meetings or whatever. My dad's on several committees and he likes to host the meetings there. Today, however, the building is filled with rows of foldaway seats. At one end there's a makeshift stage where the lots will be displayed for all to see. To the side of the stage is the lectern where my dad will stand, since he likes playing auctioneer at these events. He's even enlisted his girlfriend, Hannah, to act as the runner—or his "lovely assistant" as he refers to the role. She's tasked with fetching the items up to the stage and holding them up for everyone to see, unless of course they're too heavy and then he'll just get one of the members of staff to do it. I think he's just given Hannah the job to try to involve her so she doesn't feel left out. Normally they'd be playing golf on a Saturday, but she got compensated for the inconvenience because my dad bought her a new dress for the occasion.

Dad is dressed up in all his finery, wearing a formal morning suit as if he's having a day at the races, and since he insisted I wear a suit for the occasion, I twisted his arm for a whole new outfit from Herbert's of Mayfair. I have my own personal shopper there called Alex. Alex fitted me out in navy slim-leg trousers and a sharply-cut cream linen jacket. He teamed these with a patterned slub-silk shirt and a pair of navy Oxford brogues in a highly-reflective patent leather. It's not an outfit I'd wear every day, but for a formal occasion like this it's about as casual as I can get away with. It portrays me as the fresh young face of polite society, which is exactly how my dad likes me to be presented at these events.

I can only pray this year's dinner date won't be as painful as last year's. Frankly, I'd rather drown myself in a sick bucket than entertain Emily Wilson again, so I was ecstatic to hear the news of her recent engagement to an aircraft technician in the RAF. My guess is this year I'll be playing host to Saffron Montgomery. Dad and Lady Montgomery have been conspiring to get Saffron and I together for some time now. They always ensure we're sat next to each other at social events. Saffron is a bit giggly but survivable, if I can keep it down to two hours, tops.

I gawk out of the window, lost in despairing thoughts, as the stable yard parking bays begin to fill with high-end Mercs and SUVs. All the usual faces are here—The Whittingstalls from Cambridge; the Motsons of Bury St.Edmonds; the Tates from Mildenhall; the Johnsons from Lincoln; and, as expected, Lady Montgomery has travelled here from Norwich. She's a widow, so she's come alone. The ladies rarely bring their daughters with them. I imagine it's as embarrassing for the daughters as it is for me to have our parents trying to act as matchmakers. There are many others I recognise but can't put a name to, and even more that I've never seen before. These auctions seem to draw a bigger crowd each year.

I do the obligatory meet-and-greet thing with my dad and then, once everyone's seated, a brochure in one hand and a glass of champagne in the other, I take the chance to slip out. There's still another fifteen minutes before the auction begins and as I'm the last lot, there's plenty of time before I'm needed back here again.

7 – MACKENZIE

I hired a Bentley GT for the journey to Norfolk. It cost me thick end of a grand, but at least I look the part. I am, after all, here to make an impression on a certain young man.

After the 140-mile journey I finally arrive in Foxwell village mid-morning—at 11:10 to be precise. I pull over by the simple stone church at the end of a row of cottages. This is all that's left of that once-thriving farming community. According to the SatNav, the manor house is located a half-mile north of this tiny settlement. The auction starts in twenty minutes so my timing is about perfect despite getting stuck behind a tractor on these narrow country lanes.

It's a beautiful August morning, the sun beating down, so I get out of the car and suck in the floral-scented country air. The skies here are vast, the land flat, the space overwhelming, and there's no sign of life, apart from the noisy chatterings of birds in the trees. On the grass verge, I spot a faded sign pointing north with *Foxwell Manor* barely etched into it. I glance up the road but all I can see is thick woodland, masking the manor house from view. I can't help wondering what a young man like Aiden does for entertainment in this bucolic idyll. I'm sure I'd die of boredom within a week.

Conscious of the time, I grab my suit jacket off the hanger in the back of the car and shrug it on, and then I slide back into the driver's seat. I grab my tie from out of the glovebox and slip that on too before checking my reflection in the rear-view mirror. I grunt my approval, adjust the mirror back to its correct position, and then set off towards the woodland up ahead.

I soon locate the entrance to Foxwell Manor via an impressive set of wrought iron gates. They are flung wide open with a sign pinned to the railings.

Foxwell August Charity Auction. Today in the stable block. Ticket holders only.

I don't have a physical ticket but I was obliged to pre-register to attend so I assume they emailed me some kind of e-ticket. I enter the grounds, trying my best to stick to the tediously slow 20mph speed limit as I head on up the long driveway. Every now and then I see a side track branching off and it occurs to me that I'm not even sure where exactly the old stable block is located, but hopefully there'll be more signage up ahead.

The tall poplar trees either side of the driveway block out most of the sunlight, but not all. It flickers through the leafy overhead canopy and my eyes struggle to adjust to the constant switch between bright light and shade. Just as I approach a sweeping bend in the drive, an open-top Aston Martin shoots out of nowhere, its garish orange colour heaping more strain on my eyeballs. The car zooms past in the opposite direction, clearly ignoring the speed limit I have been so diligently sticking to. I only catch a brief glimpse of the driver, but I'm pretty sure it was Aiden Foxwell at the wheel, which is a bit worrying as he's the whole reason I'm here.

I follow the bend round a spectacular fountain in full flow and it's then I catch my first glimpse of the Grade II listed manor house. Before it's fully revealed to me, I'm diverted off to the right by security people in hi-viz jackets, directing me towards a parking bay outside the converted stable block.

Once parked, I make my way inside, where my ID is checked against my pre-registration details. I also have to sign a form promising to pay for any auction I successfully bid on. It's suggested that payments are made by bank transfer to avoid credit card fees being deducted from the charity's takings. I already had to pay fifty pounds to register as an attendee, so all the details are already set up on my account and the funds waiting. I imagine this is going to turn out to be a very expensive trip, but as they say, you have to speculate to accumulate.

These events must be a nightmare to organise. Aside from all the security aspects surrounding a wealthy family, the money laundering issue must raise its ugly head these days, since charity donations can be a means of gaining legal tax relief on illegal funds. These are, no doubt, the reasons why only those who have pre-registered can attend the auction. The Foxwell's security team will have performed background checks on everyone. Of course, all the information I provided is fully verifiable. I listed my occupation as freelance art historian and gave the address for my website. It's not like the good old days of the garden fête at the vicarage, where you could simply turn up and put your hand in your pocket.

Once my driving licence is checked against my pre-registration details, I'm presented with a bidding paddle and a brochure detailing all the lots. The brochure is a bit superfluous since I'm only here to bid on one lot and I've already spent hours online, poring over every detail of his life.

From what I can work out, Aiden Somerton Foxwell probably gets away with a lot more than he should on account of his mother being dead and him being an only child. His mother was killed in a traffic accident seven years ago. A hit-and-run incident that was never solved.

Rumour has it that the marriage of Lord and Lady Foxwell had been on rocky ground for a number of years before her death. As is typical with the upper classes, they married for the benefits each could offer the other. That's not to say they didn't love each other, but it would have been a secondary consideration. Although Lord Foxwell owns a stately home, it was his wife who brought most of the money to the table. She came from a family of wealthy bankers. It was a classic case of old money marrying new money. *She* wanted the prestige that came with being the lady of the manor, whereas *he* wanted access to her capital for the upkeep of the property. Like me, the upper classes have little time for sentiment. In fact, ever since his wife's untimely death, Lord Foxwell has been on a sexual rampage, enjoying a string of affairs with much younger women.

Not that I'm a cynic or anything, but I could be forgiven for imagining the lord had his wife bumped off. Or perhaps that's being unkind to the poor old rich bastard with the girlfriend who's twenty years his junior. Okay, maybe I'm a tad jealous. Hannah Reece is a bit of a stunner and the old man is probably in even better shape than I am. But then I suppose he has to spend a lot of time at the gym to keep up with his young fillies.

I flip straight to the back page of the brochure and there it is. *Lot 19.* A dinner date with none other than Aiden Foxwell.

I glance up at the tall silver-haired gent who just handed me the brochure. He's wearing a tag that says: *Emrys Hughes – Security Assistant.*

"Good morning, Emrys."

"How's it going, my friend?" he replies, an engaging smile suddenly lighting up his face. Considering his formal dress suit and the way he was almost standing to attention a moment ago, I hadn't been expecting such a cordial response.

"Wasn't that Aiden I just saw leaving in an Aston Martin? Had his foot to the floor. Looked like he was going somewhere in a hurry."

"Foot to the floor, you say?" Emrys rolls his eyes and shakes his head disapprovingly. "Well, I'm not going to lie to you, it probably was him. We've begged him to drive carefully until we're blue in the face, but you know how it is when you're that age. It goes in one ear and out the other."

If I'm not mistaken, I detect the lyrical inflection of a Welsh accent. I love a Welsh accent. My grandparents used to live near Aberystwyth.

"Won't he miss the auction?" I enquire, concerned I might have had a wasted journey.

Emrys crooks his finger at me, indicating for me to step to one side, so we're away from the prying ears of the other people who are signing in. "I wouldn't worry too much about it. He's probably just letting off a bit of steam before proceedings get underway," he says in a low voice.

"Does he not like these events?" I enquire, fishing for information. I'd love to know if there's been a disagreement between father and son. All such information could be useful to me when I'm trying to get my foot in the door.

"I'm sure he likes them well enough," Emrys replies tactfully. "As much as you or I would have at his age."

"So not at all then," I jest but Emrys doesn't take the bait. I change tack, thinking that if I start off on safer ground Emrys might drop his guard when we switch back to discussing Aiden. "Which part of Wales are you from?"

He grunts. "Well now, you soon picked up on that. I was raised near Brecon, on a tenanted farm, but as it happens it wasn't the life for me. I'm more of the indoorsy type. So anyhow, I went to work in the gift shop at Picton Castle and that was me ruined. I'd got a taste for it, you see. Ever since then I've moved from one stately home to another, until I ended up here. It's hard to go back once you've seen how the other half lives, isn't it?"

"Yes, I imagine it is."

"Been here five years now and I'm hoping it'll see me through to retirement. I've never been a city boy. How about you?"

"I do like the culture and nightlife of London, but I'd give it all up for a tropical island in the sun."

Emrys huffs. "Never left these shores, my friend, and never intend to." He leans in closer. "About Aiden."

36

"Yes?" I say in an enthusiastic whisper, hoping he's about to reveal a juicy piece of gossip.

"I wouldn't mention to his father that Aiden has left the building," Emrys cautions. "No point dropping the boy in it. I've every confidence he'll be back before he's missed." He pauses for a moment. "Fingers crossed."

"I suppose we were all a bit rebellious at his age," I offer.

"Yes, but not many of us had a DB11 we could take our frustrations out on. If I'd had access to that much horsepower at his age I doubt I'd be speaking with you now."

"It does seem a bit reckless of his father to let Aiden play around in that thing," I agree.

"Well, *I* wouldn't want to risk it, but Aiden knows how to get what he wants and his father needs to keep Aiden onside if he's ever to marry him off, if you know what I mean." Emrys taps the side of his nose to indicate he'll say no more on that subject. Still, it doesn't stop me digging for other information.

"I suppose driving a fast car is a better way of relieving stress than, say, drink or drugs."

Emrys shrugs. "Not being funny, but if you ask me he'd be safer knocking back a few pints than driving around in that thing. He wrapped his last car around a tree."

"Really?" *That didn't come up in my research.*

"Yes. Halfway up the drive. Keep an eye out when you leave. You'll see which tree it is. He nearly felled the damn thing. Between you and me, I'm convinced he did it on purpose. Didn't like his previous model, see. He was desperate for an upgrade."

Ooh! Naughty boy, Aiden. "Is that so? And have you considered pre-emptive action to avoid a repeat performance?"

"What do you mean? Taking his car off him?" Emrys shakes his head violently. "I doubt even his father's brave enough to attempt that."

"Actually, I was thinking more along the lines of getting a tree feller in to clear the decks, just to be on the safe side."

Emrys chuckles at my little joke. "Good idea. I'll get onto it straight away. Anyhow, you'd better go on through now or you'll miss the start. Do you have your heart set on any particular lot?"

"Well, not exactly my heart, but let's just say I have a keen interest."

"And you're not letting on which one it is."

I grin at Emrys. "Certainly not. I play my cards close to my chest."

"Very good plan," he says with a wink. He wraps an arm around my shoulder and ushers me towards a table bearing canapés and glasses of champagne. I shake my head to the proffered plate of nibbles, but readily accept a glass of the champagne. "Take a seat, my friend," Emrys says. "The auction will begin shortly. And may I wish you the very best of luck."

I incline my head in thanks, knowing full well he wouldn't be wishing me luck if he knew my intentions.

8 – AIDEN

I arrive back in the auction room with Lot 17 of 19 well underway. My dad is clearly enjoying himself. He's waving the gavel in the air like an old pro, his cheeks afire with enthusiasm as he whips up the crowd to dig deep in their pockets. Lot 17 is two weeks' use of our luxury villa in Tuscany. The eventual winners are the Johnsons who secure the lot for the bargain sum of five thousand pounds.

Dad moves swiftly on to the next lot.

"Lot 18 is this delightful pair of Yuan dynasty vases with the typical blue underglaze. What am I bid for these?"

Delightful! He hates those vases. My dad is such a hypocrite. He's hated them from the moment Mum brought them home from the antiques fair. She would never have allowed them to be sold and it feels a bit of a betrayal of her memory, but I bite my tongue and say nothing.

"Can we start the bidding at two thousand pounds?" He points the gavel at the lady sitting in the centre of the front row. "What about you, Jennifer? Come along, my lovely, these would look simply marvellous in your conservatory."

"I'm afraid they'd clash with my colour scheme," Jennifer Motson replies.

"Then redecorate, my dear," he suggests.

She smiles but declines, so he casts his gaze over the rest of the assembled crowd. "I'll take a thousand, just to get you started. Come along, ladies and gents. Remember this is for charity."

The crowd gazes back at him blankly.

"Sally-Ann, your mother would love these," he says, pointing to a lady at the back.

"Five hundred," she calls out.

"Five hundred I'm bid. Do I see six hundred anywhere?"

Another hand shoots up. "Thank you to the gentleman in the middle row. I have six hundred. Sally-Ann, seven hundred?"

She thinks about it for a second then nods.

"Seven hundred I'm bid."

The gentleman shakes his head to indicate no further bid will be forthcoming from him.

"Any advance on seven hundred? I'll take seven-and-a-half, if anyone's interested. No? Okay then, seven hundred it is. Going once, going twice. Fair warning." The gavel falls. "Sold to the lady at the back."

Finally, it's my turn. I'm the last lot. A private dinner date with the heir to Foxwell Manor. Supposedly the highlight of the event.

Dad insists I take my place up on the makeshift stage so the ladies can get a good look at what they're bidding on if I'm to be hosting one of their daughters for an evening. Of course, most of them know me already, so I find this part hugely embarrassing. I just want it to be over with.

"And now we come to the moment you've all been waiting for." Dad points his gavel at me. "A champagne dinner date with this fine young man. Come on, ladies, don't be shy. Your daughters are relying on you to secure this date for them. So, who is going to be the lucky young lady? Let's find out, shall we? Who's going to start me off?"

When the bidding begins, I cast my eyes down and concentrate on my shoe laces, not wanting to look any of them in the eye and give them a false impression that I might be encouraging them to bid.

As I expected, Lady Helena Montgomery demonstrates how keen she is to pair me off with Saffron by counter-bidding every time someone tries to outbid her. She opened up with a bid of two thousand, but competition is fierce this year and the bid now stands at six thousand, with Lady Montgomery clinging on as the highest bidder. I wish I could tell her it's a complete waste of money.

"Are we all done?" my dad asks, gavel raised, ready to seal the deal.

9 – MACKENZIE

I'm proud to call myself a thief, but it's not a career choice that would suit many people, even though there are plenty of idiots out there who think they've got what it takes to have a go. The problem stems from the way this profession has been romanticised in the movies. People think all you need is a mask and a daredevil attitude and you're good to go. This inaccurate depiction has attracted the wrong sort to the profession—the ones who think the expression "as thick as thieves" refers to the intellect level required to do the job. I can picture them scouring the online bookstores in search of *The Numbnut's Guide to Thieving*. Needless to say such a title does not exist, but imagine how this reflects on the rest of the profession when these morons get caught and have to stand trial. The first thing the prosecution is going to do is present *Exhibit A: Internet search history of the defendant*.

For the record, there are two essential requirements for being a good thief. Number one is intelligence. This definitely isn't an occupation for the dim-witted. You need to exercise due diligence, researching and studying your intended target, and you must be capable of calculating risk. Sometimes you have to make an on-the-spot judgement as to whether the article is genuine and therefore actually worth stealing. You also have to have the nous to figure out a way around the security set up.

The second qualification you need—and this is

equally important—is a natural flair for it. What do I mean by that? Well, you need to be a lying and conniving prick, unscrupulous to the core, able to pat yourself on the back as you swindle others out of their prized possessions, knowing you'll still sleep like a baby at night. If you're burdened with compassion for your fellow man, forget it. Go get yourself a job at Citizen's Advice.

So you see, unlike the way it's depicted in the movies, this profession is neither glamorous nor heroic. It's actually a very studious and lonely profession, and needless to say we're an unsocial bunch. We don't meet up regularly or do Christmas shows like the Magic Circle, but we do have one thing in common with them. We never reveal our sleight of hand.

It's not like we wouldn't love to brag about it if we could because every thief is a born show-off. The problem is, if we went around boasting about how we exploited the flaws in your security system, you'd just get them fixed. This is the only downside to the job—the fact we don't get to rub your noses in it once we've relieved you of your most precious assets. We'd love to publicly ridicule you for believing you actually had everything safely under lock and key, but instead we have to skulk off and keep a low profile if we don't wish to get caught. That part really pisses me off.

So if there's no *How To* guide, how does a thief learn his trade? Well, as I've already indicated, it's down to aptitude, attitude and the size of your organ. Not *that* organ. The one in your skull. And, as with any other ancient profession, a tip or two from an old master never goes amiss. Oh, did I not mention my dad was a thief, God rest him? I suppose that's how I got into it in the first place.

Mum passed when I was a small boy, so there was just me and my dad, and it was the only way he knew to put food on the table. He liked sparkly things. I've never been a fan of jewellery myself. I hate things that are just *pretty* with no real function. Personally, I prefer things that talk to me and tell a story. Something with depth that I can study a hundred times over and still discover a new facet, or a different nuance that I hadn't noticed before. That's why art is my thing. I love art. You have to love it to be good at stealing it. You have to make yourself an expert in the field so you know what it is you're actually looking at and whether it's worth the risk. This isn't a profession so much as a vocation. It's what I was born to do.

I wish my old dad could see me now. He was never very free with his affections, but I'm sure I'd see a spark of pride in his eyes. I loved my old man, even though he was a crotchety old cunt, but if I'm honest he was nothing more than a bumbling fool in comparison to how I operate. I'm surprised he never got caught. But I *will* give him credit for teaching me what is probably the most valuable lesson a thief could ever learn. *Don't be a headline chaser.* In other words, never steal anything so famous and loved by the public that stealing it would create a media storm. A mention in the local rag is fine but you don't want your story picked up by the nationals because then the police feel the need to apply serious manpower to solving the crime. Typically, they don't have anywhere near the necessary resources to solve workaday robberies, hence the soundness of my dad's advice and why I've stuck to it all these years.

I've still made a decent living out of it because we live in a world where high-end cars can cost six-figure sums, so you'd have to steal something worth several million to get noticed. To date, I've never stolen anything worth more than half a million, and usually much less, which means that at the ten percent going rate on the black market, I typically earn between £20k and £50k per heist. You don't have to do many of those a year to make a good living off this line of work. I've already stashed enough away that I could retire to a nice house in the country, but at thirty-three years of age I'm not quite ready for my pipe and slippers just yet.

I guess that's how I've ended up here, trying to engineer my way into Foxwell Manor with a view to stealing a Raphael. I've realised that a "comfortable" retirement isn't going to be enough for me. What I actually want is to retire stinking rich. So for this one last roll of the dice the rule book is getting tossed out of the window. I'm going to go out in style. And all I need to get my foot in the door is to win a dinner date with young Foxwell. It couldn't be simpler.

The auction seems interminable. The only thing that's caught my eye so far is the sexy young lady holding up the lots. If I'm not mistaken that willowy blonde in the frothy yellow dress is Lord Foxwell's girlfriend, Hannah Reece. *Lucky old bastard!*

Finally we get to Lot 19.

"Here we go," I mutter under my breath when it's announced. I can only assume Aiden must have made it back from his little spin in his

Aston Martin. Then it's confirmed as he climbs up onto the makeshift stage, accompanied by gigglish mutterings from the ladies in the audience. He really does cut a fine figure of a young man. Dressed in a fetching navy-and-cream ensemble, he looks the epitome of youthful sartorial elegance. All those online photos I studied really didn't do him justice. He has an almost exotic look about him with his dark wavy hair, tanned skin and luscious red lips. I swear he gazes straight at me for a second, but then he looks away and stares at the ground, hands clasped behind his back, seemingly embarrassed by the whole affair. And who can blame him?

"And now we come to the moment you've all been waiting for." Lord Foxwell points his gavel at his son. "A champagne dinner date with this fine young man. Come on, ladies, don't be shy."

I sit back and bide my time, watching the hands shoot in the air. One lady in particular seems determined to see off all the competition. The bidding finally settles at six thousand pounds, with the persistent lady being the top bidder. She glances around nervously as if she's at the limit of what she's prepared to bid and is praying there are no further counter-offers.

"Going once. Going twice. Are we all done?" Lord Foxwell asks, raising his gavel in the air, about to award the win to the overzealous lady near the front.

I jump to my feet. "Let's not mess around here, ladies. Let's make it a nice round ten."

Everyone turns around to gawk at me and even Aiden lifts his head to stare at me like I've gone stark raving bonkers.

"S...sorry?" Lord Foxwell stutters. "Are you bidding, sir?"

I give him a smug grin. "I am. The bid is ten thousand pounds."

"Er...well, thank you, sir. That's...exceedingly generous." He switches his gaze from me to the lady I'm bidding against. "I'm afraid the bid is ten thousand, Helena. Dare I ask, any advance, my dear?"

She shakes her head vigorously and then twists around to glare at me.

Lord Foxwell casts his gaze over the whole crowd. "Any advance on ten thousand?" I hear mumblings but no further counter-bid is forthcoming. With such an extravagant overbid, Lord Foxwell doesn't hang around. He slams his gavel down hard. "Sold to the gentleman. Your daughter is going to be a very happy young lady," he assures me. I say nothing, simply holding up my paddle so he can take a note of the number, and then I make my way over to the lady at the payment desk. I quickly make the bank transfer over the phone and show the lady that it's been processed at my end. Then she hands me a form to fill in. It has all my registration details auto-completed on the first page, but there's an additional page attached with questions specific to Lot 19.

I run my gaze down the list which includes questions about food allergies, food preferences and drink preferences. I also have to tick my preferred attendance date from the list of four options; the earliest being in three weeks' time, on the first Friday in September. The sooner the better, as far as I'm concerned.

I pull my Aspinal rollerball pen from my inside jacket pocket, ready to work my way down the list. The very first question at the top of the sheet brings a wicked smile to my lips.

Name of person attending the dinner date.

I know Lord Foxwell assumes I have a daughter in the wings, keen to spend an evening with his son, but I'm afraid he's going to be in for a bit of a shock. The blank box, where I'm supposed to enter the young lady's name, stretches across the full width of the page, no doubt so there's also room to accommodate her title. I press the nib of my pen to the paper and scrawl a single-word response.

Oneself.

10 – AIDEN

I know when I'm summoned to my dad's study that I'm in trouble, but for once I don't have a clue what I've done wrong. I went through with the annual charity charade, as expected of me, so what can he possibly have to grouse about now? I slump into the leather armchair across the desk from him. He ignores me at first, seemingly absorbed in the notes he's reading.

"Is this going to take long?" I sigh, letting Dad know I'm bored before we've even begun. "I was hoping to go out for a drive?"

He lifts his gaze. I can tell by the grizzly look on his face that I'm about to get chewed up and spat out. "Did *you* put him up to this?"

I fold my arms and glare at him. "Did I put *who* up to *what*?"

"You know perfectly well what I'm referring to. Sit up straight, boy."

I roll my eyes but decide it's best to obey, considering his foul mood. I uncross my arms and shuffle in my seat, adopting a more upright posture.

"I wait all year to auction you off to a young lady and you arrange for some idiot bloke to outbid the lot of them so he can put *himself* forward as your dinner date. The arrogance of the man, to parade your sexuality in front of everyone."

"I thought you said he'd bid on behalf of his daughter."

"That was my mistaken assumption," Dad freely admits. "But then I read the forms he filled out." He shuffles the papers in his hands until he finds the right one and points at it. "It says it right here in black-and-white. *'Name of person attending the dinner date: Oneself.'*"

I snort out a laugh. "Really? Show me." I reach across the desk but Dad slaps my hand away.

"This isn't funny, Aiden."

"Well, *I* think it is," I reply, unable to wipe the smirk off my face.

"So you admit you put him up to this?"

"Me? No. This has nothing to do with me."

Despite my protestations, it's clear from the ensuing rant that my dad still doesn't believe me.

"I despair of you, Aiden, I really do. Imagine the questions I'm going to face the next time I see the ladies. They'll all be keen to know how your dinner date went. What am I supposed to tell them? How could you do this to me? All you had to do is try to get on with a young lady for one night of the year. Is that too much to ask? You could have taken her up to your room, done the deed, and got it over with. You can sneak out to see your gentlemen friends any other night of the year."

"Done the deed!" I shriek, shifting to the edge of my seat so I'm closer to my dad as I prepare to pour scorn on his comment. "There are several things wrong with that sentence. First off, it's supposed to be a dinner date. No-one said anything about taking her up to my room. That's not part of the bargain. Secondly, even if I took her to my room, it wouldn't be to *do the deed*. I don't sleep with girls. Get over it. Thirdly, even if we did the deed, both she and I, being responsible adults, would take the necessary precautions because *getting her pregnant* on a first date is never going to be a good idea, even if such a thing were physically possible, which is highly unlikely."

"What would you know about it?" my dad grunts.

"Whatever! If you think this is any way to go about continuing the family line, then I pity you." Dad gawks at me in silence and I heave a sigh, sitting back in my chair, adopting a less confrontational posture. "Look, Dad. I have no idea who that guy was. I've never seen him before in my life."

"Then we're in even more trouble than I thought."

"Trouble? Why? What do you mean?"

"I've just been going through his details and apparently he's very interested in art."

"Oh and that's a crime now, is it?" I scoff. "Do you think just because he's cultured I'll automatically want to jump his bones?"

"Don't be vulgar. I meant that he may be using you to get to my art collection."

"What!"

Dad points to another of the sheets of paper in his hand. "He lists his occupation as freelance art historian. Don't you think that's a bit of a coincidence, considering what I've got hanging on the walls?"

"Oh thanks, Dad!" I sneer. "So you think he bid ten thousand pounds for a night with me simply because he wants to admire your stupid artwork. Well, that shows what a low opinion you have of

53

me."

"Not *admire* it, Aiden. *Steal* it."

I screw my nose up, wondering where on earth he gets these weird notions. "Get real, Dad."

"Well, if he's a thief he's hardly going to include that in his bloody résumé, is he?" Dad leans forward, resting his elbows on the desk, and gazing straight at me, concern etched across his face. "The thing is, Aiden, the last one I acquired cost me an awful lot of money."

"Oh, so that's why you're so paranoid about your collection all of a sudden. And may I ask how much *an awful lot* is?"

Dad sighs and leans back in his chair making the leather creak. "A breathtaking amount. It's a very important piece."

"Who's the artist?"

"I'd rather not say."

I huff. "I can always go upstairs and look."

"It's unsigned."

I gawk at him. "You wasted a big chunk of *my* inheritance on an *unsigned* painting?"

"It's genuine. I've had it verified."

"Who by? Dodgy Daniel?" I scoff. My dad has some very dubious associates who are connected to the criminal underworld; none more so than Dodgy Daniel, as I like to refer to him.

Dad's face turns crimson. "By an associate of his, and it's not your bloody inheritance until I kick the bucket and that isn't happening anytime soon."

"Well, you look like you're about to have a heart attack to me."

He draws in a long breath and slowly exhales. "Look, Aiden, I didn't exactly obtain the painting by legal methods, if you catch my drift."

"No shit! I figured that much if Dodgy Daniel was involved. So are you saying you acquired it on the black market?"

He gawks at me. "What do *you* know about black market trading?"

I chuckle at his undue concern. "Chill, Dad. Everything I know I discovered from watching movies. You say it's a waste of time but it's the best education in life I've ever had."

"That isn't life. It's fiction. You need to get your head out of that fantasy world you live in and start acting like you belong in the real world."

I grunt. "What for? So I can find myself a respectable young lady?"

"Yes, exactly that."

"No thanks!" I sneer.

"All I'm saying is you need to be on your guard when there are strangers in the house. I can't insure the painting without a legitimate receipt, so you see what an awkward position this puts me in, especially when this complete stranger has coughed up ten grand to gain access to the house. It strikes me as extremely odd."

"To gain access to *me*, Dad," I remind him. "He paid for a dinner date with *me*, not your bloody painting. I'm a valuable commodity too, as you're fond of reminding me. Anyway, if you're that worried about the painting, put it in the closet. You don't have to have it on display for everyone to see."

"Put it in the closet!" my dad repeats in a voice that tells me he's not too enamoured with that idea. "Don't be an idiot, boy. Why do you think I invested in that state-of-the-art laser security system? The safest place for it is on the wall."

"Well then, you have nothing to worry about."

"Nothing's foolproof, Aiden."

I smirk at him. "No, Dad, not even your little scheme to marry me off. I can't believe a man bid for me. That's hilarious!" My dad clearly isn't amused so I promptly switch back to discussing the painting. "Why don't you take your precious piece of art and put it in a safety deposit box at the bank. Then you can stop worrying about it. Out of sight, out of mind."

"Why should I? I don't want it out of sight. I paid a lot of money for it. I want to be able to look at it when the mood takes me."

"Which is never," I mutter under my breath, knowing full well the only thing that holds my dad's attention these days is Hannah Reese—his latest lady friend who's only ten years older than me. I get to my feet and begin heading to the door, speaking over my shoulder as I go. "However, it is duly noted that you're more concerned about your stupid artwork than whether or not I intend to get my rocks off with the handsome gent who bid on me."

Dad shouts after me. "Don't even think about taking him upstairs, Aiden. You know you're banned from taking men to your room."

"No worries." I turn around when I reach the door so I can leave my dad with one last thought. "I'll probably let him screw me over the dining table," I taunt, my chin tilted up in defiance. "After all, he'll want his money's worth. And ten grand is one hell of a fuck."

Dad mutters something unrepeatable under his breath and jumps to his feet. I scarper, making a run for it up the corridor, Dad chasing after me. I head for Frankie's office. The last time I got into serious trouble was when I deliberately crashed my car into a tree so I could get an upgrade. I remember how Dad wanted to throttle me that day, but as our head of security, one of Frankie's main duties is to act as my bodyguard. It's his job to see that the heir to the family fortune comes to no harm. Since my mum died, Frankie has become sort of a second dad to me. He spends more time fretting about my welfare than my real dad.

I'm surprised how fit my dad is. He's been spending a lot of time down the gym lately, getting all muscly for his lady friend. He almost catches up with me, but I manage to dive into Frankie's office ahead of him. Frankie looks up from his computer screen and gawks at me. I screech to a halt just behind Frankie, standing at his right shoulder, as my dad enters. Dad halts a couple of paces in. We're both panting. Frankie switches his gaze between us but says nothing. It's a fairly regular occurrence for me to use him as a bulwark against my dad's temper. As easy as it is for my dad to lose his cool, he still hates to cause a scene in front of the staff.

I plead my innocence. "Come on, Dad, you know I was only joking."

He huffs. "Except it wasn't very bloody funny, was it? You know better than to speak to me like that."

"Sorry. I'm just edgy from that stupid auction. I need to blow some steam off, that's all. I'll be good as gold once I've been out for a drive."

"You'd better be because I'll wash your mouth out with carbolic soap if I hear any more filthy talk like that from you."

I screw my nose up. "Carbolic soap? What the hell's that?"

"Nasty stuff," Frankie informs me. "My dad used to use it. I can smell it now." He shudders. "Makes my skin crawl."

"Yes, get some on order, Frankie," my dad says by way of a threat aimed at me.

"Yes, sir," Frankie replies.

My dad wags his finger at me. "And don't think I don't know where you're planning on going for your little drive. I'm not so dumb as you'd like me to be, young man."

I scowl at my dad, wondering if he's bluffing or if he really *does* know about my little trips to Kelly and Grant's place. It wouldn't surprise me. He has spies everywhere reporting back to him. I went to a gay bar once and he knew about that the next day.

"Be back by teatime," my dad instructs me.

"Sure."

Dad leaves and I heave a sigh of relief, exchanging a glance with Frankie.

"Tough day?" Frankie asks.

"Yes, Frankie. A very tough day. I need all the data you have on the man who won the dinner date with me."

Frankie gives me a quirky look. "Oh, is that what this is about?"

I nod. "Whoever he is, he's dropped me right in it."

"Mackenzie Oden," Frankie informs me.

"Oh, is that his name? Dad's been going through his notes with a fine toothcomb, no doubt trying to find some connection between us, except there isn't one. I don't need a hard copy, just send me the link to his file."

"Certainly, sir. Just a second."

I've told Frankie a million times he can call me Aiden, but he still insists on calling me "sir" so I let it wash over me these days. He taps away on his keyboard for a few seconds and then looks up at me. "There. Done. You should have it now."

"Thanks. I'll check it out later. I hope this Mackenzie person knows what he's letting himself in for. I'm going out now. I'll see you later."

"Enjoy your drive, sir."

"I will."

Just as I reach the door, Frankie offers up a parting comment that he knows will get my hackles up. "Drive carefully."

I halt in my tracks and turn around to face him. I can see the twinkle of amusement in his eyes. On the surface he always acts strictly professional, but he loves to tease me in this underhand kind of way whenever the opportunity presents itself. I think it's his version of digging me in the ribs, the way friends do when they're joshing with each other. He already knows what my response is going to be.

"Stop mothering me, Frankie."

"Yes, sir," he says with a soft smirk.

During the six mile trip over to Kelly and Grant's place I can't stop thinking about the auction. Imagine some man I've never heard of turning up at my dad's charity auction and bidding on me in front of everyone. Who does he think he is, stirring things up like that? Dad's clearly furious and believes I put him up to it.

I can guarantee Dad's going to be watching us like a hawk when this Mackenzie person turns up next month for the dinner date, especially since he thinks Mackenzie is interested in his art collection. Of course, that's just my dad being paranoid, but I could do without all the extra grief.

If Mackenzie Oden thinks I'm going to roll over for him, he's got another thing coming. He might have paid ten grand for the pleasure of my company, but what he's actually going to get is ten grand's worth of ingratitude for putting me in this awkward situation.

11 – MACKENZIE

It's the night of the dinner date. I decided against hiring a car this time, choosing instead to relax on the train. That got me as far as King's Lynn and then I grabbed a taxi outside the station. It's just pulled up to Foxwell Manor. I pay the driver and ask if he can come and pick me up in three hours. I'll adjust the pickup time later if needs be. I've no idea how long the date is supposed to last but it didn't come with an offer of a room for the night, so I've booked a hotel on the coast, a twenty-minute drive away.

The taxi disappears up the drive and I'm left standing outside the grand front entrance, scarcely able to believe this day has finally arrived. It seems like an age since I was last here to bid on the auction, although it's actually only been three weeks. I gaze up at the half-timbered building, a beautifully preserved example of Tudor architecture. Together with the brooding skies overhead, it's a spooky aesthetic. I think about all the generations of Foxwells that have lived and died here and wonder if their ghostly apparitions ever roam these premises after dark. It's the sort of venue that could host a murder mystery weekend very effectively. You could scare everyone to death simply by turning the lights off.

A chill breeze whips up from nowhere, my thin summer suit offering scant protection from it, and I shudder as I press the doorbell and stand back. Thankfully, I'm not kept waiting long.

"Hi there!" I blurt out somewhat in shock. I wasn't expecting Aiden to answer the door personally. He's looking very edible this evening, dressed in dark tight-fitting trousers and a white open-neck shirt.

"Good evening," he replies, his voice deeper than I imagined it would be. "If I'm not mistaken you're my dinner date."

"You're not mistaken," I confirm.

We smile at each other politely, for longer than feels natural or comfortable, his smiling eyes boring into mine.

"Can I come in?" I eventually ask.

He drops the smile and stares at me pointedly. "Really? You wish to enter?" he says in an incredulous tone.

"Sorry, what have I missed? Was I supposed to come bearing gifts or something?"

He doesn't reply, choosing instead to fold his arms across his chest. *Oh God, no, not the silent treatment.* I haven't even set foot inside the place yet and already this feels like a date with a certain lady friend I know.

"Yes I wish to enter."

"No."

"No?" I scowl at him, wishing I knew the rules to this silly game. "Look, I've had a very long journey and I'm sure you don't need reminding of the ten grand I coughed up for the pleasure of your company this evening."

"Who said it would be a pleasure?"

"Well it's sort of implied," I point out. "You don't go on a date expecting to have a godawful time, now do you?"

"You know my dad was expecting you to be a woman."

"I'm not here to see your father."

"But I'm the one who's had to put up with his wrath over the past few weeks since you outbid Lady Montgomery."

Oh, so that's why he's miffed. "Tell him I'll wear a dress if it makes him feel better."

"I think it's the bit *under* the dress that concerns him."

"He shouldn't be looking up my dress."

"This really isn't funny, you know. He can be a real ogre when someone rubs him up the wrong way and you didn't even bring me a gift to compensate for what I've had to put up with on your behalf."

I decide an apology is probably in order. Not because I think I've done anything I need to apologise for, but I doubt he's going to let me in without one. "I'm sorry your father has been giving you grief because I won the auction, but I did pay a bucket load of money to his charity, so I'm entitled to expect him to look the other way if he doesn't like it. I'm also entitled to be let in at the appointed hour of our dinner date." Okay, so it's a half-hearted sort of apology but I'm getting a bit riled now, being made to stand out on the doorstep while we have this conversation. "And as for bringing you a gift, I assumed you'd have a cellar full of wine, so that seemed a pointless gesture, and I doubted very much that roses would be your thing."

Aiden quirks an eyebrow. "How presumptuous of you. I love roses."

"You have loads in your gardens," I point out.

63

"And what has that to do with anything?"

I roll my eyes and sigh, feeling exasperated. "I'll go and gather a few if it'll make you happy."

"Don't bother. You'll only get a nasty prick."

"Oh please don't concern yourself. I know how to deal with nasty pricks."

"Then perhaps you can help me out. I've got one standing on my doorstep."

That didn't come up in my research. All those hours I spent poring over his background details and nowhere did it say he was a smart-mouthed little shit.

"Are you going to let me in or not?" I snap.

"Did you leave your manners at home?"

"Yes they're in my other suit pocket, along with my patience, so how about we stop playing silly buggers."

"You haven't presented yourself."

"Sorry?" I scoff.

"Name."

I take a deep breath and fiddle with my cufflink as I concentrate very hard on not losing my cool. "You must know my name. I filled out enough bloody forms to get here."

"And you think the fact you had to write your name on a form excuses you from introducing yourself?"

"I didn't realise you were going to be so *prissy* about matters of etiquette."

His lip curls. "*Prissy*?"

"Well, clearly introductions are redundant when we both know full well who the other is. Is this really the way to start our first date?"

"First date!" He snorts. "You imagine this is the first of many, do you?"

"If you play your cards right," I reply with a sarcastic smirk. "Only next time I'll wear a sweater under my suit jacket if we're going to conduct it on the doorstep."

"You can come in when you've introduced yourself and not before. I only entertain gentlemen."

"So I've heard."

He narrows his eyes at me and huffs. "I'm dying to know who put you up to this."

"Look, I know perfectly well you must have checked out every detail of my life by now, otherwise I wouldn't be here talking to you, so formal introductions seem rather superfluous when you probably already know more about me than my own mother."

"Seriously? You think that's *my* job, do you? We have security people to check out people like you."

"Like me? What's that supposed to mean?"

He presses his front teeth to his bottom lip to form the letter V and then pings the word "Visitors" at me like it's a missile aimed right between my eyes. It's so effective I actually blink.

I'm desperate to get inside, into the warm, so I decide to let him have the win. "Mackenzie Oden." I bow. "At your service, My Lord."

"Don't call me that. I don't go by any title." He steps to one side, inviting me to enter at long last. "Titles are meaningless these days. You can buy one online for twenty quid."

I cross the threshold, stepping into the hallway

with its spectacular encaustic-tiled floor in a Tudor rose design.

"Shall I call you Mr. Oden?" he asks.

I turn to face him and find myself gazing straight into a pair of huge chocolate-brown eyes. "My friends call me Mac."

He grunts. "You have friends?"

Don't sound surprised, you cheeky little runt.

Aiden turns and begins striding up the corridor, his upright frame possessing all the austere grace of a ballet dancer, while his fancy shoes clip-clop like a horse trotting on the tiles.

"Just a moment," I call out after him.

He swivels to face me "What now?"

"Name," I insist churlishly.

He glares at me. "You can't be serious."

"You haven't introduced yourself and I only dine with gentlemen."

"Are you mocking me, Mr. Oden?"

"I'm just asking for your name."

"Aiden Foxwell," he barks, staring daggers at me.

"Is that what your friends call you?"

"Don't have any," he snaps as he turns and continues on up the corridor.

"Now there's a surprise," I mutter as I follow behind, rushing to catch up with his brisk pace.

We head down the long, chilly hallway, passing several closed doors until we get to one that's slightly ajar. Aiden pushes the door open and invites me to enter ahead of him.

It's a small but beautifully presented dining room, too grand to feel intimate, but certainly impressive. I glance up at the ornate cornices and the crystal chandelier hanging above the long wooden dining table. The walls are lined with walnut panelling and there's a stone fireplace at the far end. It's noticeably warmer in this room although the fire isn't lit so there must be some kind of discreet heating system. Against the side wall there's an oak dresser with roundels carved into the wood in a geometric rose design.

On the dresser sits a silver punchbowl with eight matching cups dangling from hooks around its rim. The punchbowl isn't in use this evening. Instead there's a decanted bottle of wine waiting for us.

There are eight chairs around the dining table, although it's only been set for the two of us—at *opposite* ends of the table. We take our seats and sit in silence while the obsequious waiter faffs around pouring the wine before serving the soup, which, he informs me, is spiced parsnip.

Finally, we are left on our own.

Aiden gazes at me across the length of the table. "There are usually candles," he notes. "Someone's taken them away. My dad, I expect. He probably thought it would be too romantic."

"Bummer! I could always light a cigar if you just want something that glows."

"You're not allowed to smoke in here."

"Double bummer!"

We drop our napkins in our laps in unison and pick up our soup spoons to take a first tentative sip from the steaming bowls.

"It's delicious," I tell him.

He sets his spoon down. "You know, Mr. Oden,

it's not very nice to start a date with a lie."

"Don't you like the soup?"

"I don't mean the soup. I'm referring to what you said on the doorstep. You accused me of knowing more about you than your own mother."

"What's wrong with that?"

"You don't have a mother, so why pretend otherwise?"

An unbidden grin struts across my lips. "So you *have* boned up on me."

He colours up slightly. "I always bone up when I'm having dinner with a gentleman friend."

Did he just make a sexual innuendo or is it my filthy imagination?

"Gentleman friend? Well, if we're friends now, perhaps you'll call me Mac."

"I'll call you Mackenzie. That's your name."

A voice booms out from behind me. "You can call *me* Lord Foxwell."

Aiden's face drops and I turn around to see the imposing figure of his father standing behind me.

I get to my feet and turn to face him. Up close like this I can see the family resemblance. Lord Foxwell may well have been the spitting image of Aiden when he was younger, except now his face is lined and his wavy brown hair is greying at the temples. I'd say he's a handsome gent for someone in his fifties, except for the sneer on his lip and the look of dark contempt in his hooded eyes.

"Good evening, Lord Foxwell." I hold out my right hand, but instead of shaking it he glowers at me.

I drop my hand and he moves closer so he's

68

right in my face. He's taller than me, forcing me to look up at him and inhale the scent of roasted coffee on his hot breath. This time when he speaks, it's in a low rumble, like the distant thunder of a raging storm. "If you should wish to make a donation to my chosen charity next year, please feel free to bid on the villa in Tuscany."

Clearly, as Aiden mentioned, Lord Foxwell isn't too happy that I won the dinner date, but that's just too bad. We exchange a meaningful stare before I deign to respond. "I don't have time to play tourist."

"Okay. What about Lot 3? Surely that would have suited your tastes?"

"And what was Lot 3?"

"The statue of the young boy. The *naked* young boy."

I glare at him. I'm damned if I'm going to let the old man burst in here with his aggressive stance and his crude innuendo; not after the eye-watering sum I paid out to be here tonight. "Wasn't worth ten grand though, was it?" I sneer. "And I do so like to make my presence felt at these charity events."

"You certainly did that," he growls.

"Besides which," I continue, "I have no use for ornaments or statues. They're just clutter."

"But clearly you're partial to young boys, Mr. Oden." He spares Aiden a quick glance before refocussing his venom on me. "Particularly posh young boys, I imagine, since you're willing to fork out ten grand to get your hands on one."

My jaw stiffens. "I don't much care for your tone *or* the insinuation. The only thing I'm partial to is a consenting adult. If the 'boy' you're referring to is your son, you may be surprised to learn he's all grown up now. Maybe you were looking elsewhere when it happened. Probably at that pretty young blonde you hang around with." I pause as both he and Aiden gasp audibly at my vitriolic retort. "Your son is an adult with the right to make his own choices and if he asks me to leave I will, so please do us the courtesy of buggering off so we can dine in peace."

"How dare you speak to me like that in my own home?" he snaps.

"I paid ten grand to spend an evening enjoying good wine, good food and good company. You're spoiling my evening, Lord Foxwell. Is my money not good enough? Because if that's the case you'd better refund it immediately and then I shall go straight to the press and tell them how Lord Foxwell treats commoners who successfully bid at one of his charity auctions. I shall tell them you're not only a snob, you're a homophobic snob."

"That's a lie," he snarls, his flared nostrils looking like a double-barrelled shotgun aimed right between my eyes. "I may be a snob but I am *not* homophobic and you will not drag my family name through the gutter press. Do you understand?"

I nod. "And do you accept that I am here to dine with your son and I will only leave if Aiden wishes it?"

Lord Foxwell looks to his son. "Well, Aiden?"

"He stays," Aiden insists.

"Very well," Lord Foxwell grunts, turning to me again. "You do understand the dinner date does not extend to a room for the night, so I hope you've made alternative arrangements."

"Of course. Now, if that's all, I'll get back to my very expensive soup before it gets cold."

He huffs. "Do be careful not to choke on it." He turns to leave and I retake my seat, picking up my soup spoon just as the door slams behind me. I shake my head at Aiden. "What an arse! Is he always like that? I hope you don't turn into him when you get older."

Aiden snorts. "Oh my God, Mackenzie, that was awesome. It's so refreshing to meet someone who isn't afraid to stand up to my dad."

I'm pleased to note there's still steam coming off my bowl of soup. I lift a spoonful to my lips and blow, pausing to make a flippant remark. "I get the distinct impression your father hates me and I don't even know the man."

"That's an understatement," Aiden tells me. "He'd probably kill you if he thought he could get away with it."

I gulp hard, swallowing the soup faster than intended. It burns as it slides down my gullet. "That's charming. This whole evening is meant to be in aid of charity. I doubt that man has a single charitable bone in his body. My dinner date is starting to feel more like a game of Cluedo."

Aiden's hand stills just before his spoon reaches his mouth. "Whatever do you mean?"

"I didn't realise I was putting my life on the line when I bid at that auction. I can just imagine tomorrow's newspaper headline. It'll say, *'The old man did it, with an axe, in the dining room.'* Do you think I should be concerned?"

Aiden chuckles. "No, you'll be fine," he says

reassuringly. "An axe is too gory. There'd be blood everywhere. There are much better ways to kill a person than that. If *I* really detested someone, I'd poison their soup."

I drop my spoon and it clatters in the bowl, making a dramatic splash that soils the tablecloth. Aiden holds his napkin to his mouth as he bursts into an ungentlemanly fit of giggles.

I lean over to sniff at my bowl. "It's funny you should say that because this soup definitely smells of garlic and they *do* say arsenic has a similar smell. Did you choose the soup? Garlic seems a bit…anti-social…for a dinner date."

"No, I didn't pick the menu. Maybe my dad did." He gives me a coy smile. "The garlic may be deliberate, to put us off kissing."

"Or maybe it's there to disguise the smell of the arsenic."

He huffs. "Don't be daft. If he'd poisoned it, he'd be killing me too."

"Not if he got the waiter to add the arsenic to my bowl after the soup had been dished up."

"Relax, Mackenzie, nobody uses arsenic anymore. It's *sooo* nineteenth century," Aiden drawls, rolling his eyes dismissively. He pauses to take a sip of wine and then cocks his head on one side and gazes off into the distance, as if he's thinking. "Do you know what I'd use?"

"What for?"

"If I wanted to poison you."

We gaze at each other across the length of the table. "I'm all ears."

"I'd use thallium. It's tasteless, odourless, and slow-acting. You'd suffer a lingering death over the span of several horribly painful weeks."

I gawk at him in silence for a few moments before I recover my voice. "Thank you for those reassuring words. Do you know what, I think I'll skip the soup course, if it's all the same to you." I shove my bowl away and rub my lips with the napkin to remove any lingering drops.

"Really? I'm rather enjoying it," Aiden says, scooping up the last few mouthfuls.

I pick up my wine glass, taking a good glug of the burgundy liquid, which I swill around like a mouthwash before swallowing.

Aiden sets his spoon down and stares at me, frowning. "Are you sure you're okay, Mackenzie. You've gone quite pale."

I eye him warily. "It's slightly disconcerting that you appear to be an expert in food poisoning. This isn't the type of thing any dinner guest wishes to discover about their host."

"Sorry," he lies, his wicked grin telling me he isn't even remotely contrite. "First my dad storms in here, looking ready to throttle you, and now I've put you off your soup with talk of poisoning you. How rude we are! You must be wishing you hadn't bothered coming. It's like a dinner date at the house of horrors."

"Did you study toxicology?"

"No I just absorb all that type of thing."

My brain draws a blank trying to work out what he means. "You absorb poisons?" I ask tentatively.

Aiden screws up his face. "Oh yeah, it's like one of my superpowers," he scoffs contemptuously. "Don't be an idiot, Mackenzie. I meant I pick things up easily. I absorb information. I'm into all that kind of shit."

"Sorry. What shit?"

"Spy stuff. Poisonings, murder, mayhem. I watch a lot of films—you know, thrillers, gangster movies, film noir—anything with a dark theme and a sexy anti-hero. You get to know how things are done. I reckon I'd make a pretty good spy, if ever the British government called me up."

"Good God! I had no idea what I was getting into arranging a dinner date with you, Aiden Foxwell. You sound mad, bad and dangerous to know. Maybe I should leave while the going's good. Clearly, you're not a person to get on the wrong side of."

He rises from his seat and walks around the table, bringing his glass of wine with him. Taking the seat to my left, he looks me straight in the eyes. "You can't leave now. Not when I'm starting to like you."

I arch my eyebrows at him. "Really? I thought you couldn't stand the sight of me."

"Oh, when you first arrived you mean? That was just me getting payback for the awkward position you put me in. You saw how my dad was with you just now. Imagine what I've had to put up with ever since the auction. Anyhow, I'm going to forgive you because I liked the way you stood up to him. It was very impressive, Mackenzie. In fact, I've just decided you're going to be my new bestie."

"Bestie? That's quite a leap from being total strangers twenty minutes ago."

He nods. "I'm rather impetuous like that."

"Easy come, easy go?"

"We'll see."

"At this rate of progress we'll be married and divorced before the night is out."

He sighs. "I'm afraid you and I could never be married. Aiden Oden just doesn't work for me." He pauses for a moment. "Unless, of course, you're prepared to take *my* name."

"We could hyphenate," I offer.

"Aiden Foxwell-Oden? I don't know," he muses. "Still sounds a bit clumsy."

"So it's a deal breaker?"

He nods. "But it would solve a hell of a lot of problems for me if you could see your way clear to having my baby."

I snort. "Sorry, definitely not. Not on our first date, at least."

"But I've only got until I'm twenty-five to produce an heir, otherwise I'm disinherited. That's just two years and two months away."

"That's no time at all. You need to get your skates on, so what are you doing dining with me?"

"You bid on me, remember?"

"Oh yes. That was a bit naughty of me, wasn't it?"

"Exceptionally naughty. I believe some kind of punishment should be exacted for your sheer audacity."

"You mean other than the spiteful welcome you and your father dished out? Not to mention the fact I've already suffered a pecuniary punishment to the tune of ten thousand pounds for the 'sheer audacity' of wishing to dine with you."

"Don't be such a whiner, Mackenzie. I'm certain you can easily afford it, otherwise you wouldn't be here."

I lean forward and rest my chin on my elbow. "So tell me, My Lord, what other form of punishment does your little heart desire? Do you wish to tie me to the bedpost and flog me? Is that it?"

Aiden looks away, blushing, and I swear it's the sweetest thing I've ever seen. It makes me wonder just how many lovers he's actually had. I bet I could count them on one hand. Maybe even one finger.

"How did you know I'm gay?" he asks softly without looking up. "Only a handful of people know. Someone must have put you up to this." He looks up at me now. "Tell me. Who was it?"

I lean back and take another drink of wine while I decide how to respond. "No-one. I like to support these smaller charities."

He looks disappointed. "Was that the only reason?"

"Well, I *am* rather partial to good food and good company. And then there's your father's wine cellar. He's renowned for stocking all the best vintages, so I was hoping we'd be sampling one on our date." I raise my glass to him. "This isn't one of those, unfortunately, but it's still a sexy little number."

"How can wine be sexy?"

"It flirts with your senses and makes your toes tingle."

His mouth twists into a cocky smile. "That's not the wine. It's my proximity to you. I'll go back to my own seat."

He picks up his glass and stands. As he makes his way back to the other end of the table, I observe him with lustful appreciation for his youthful form. I make a soft growl in my throat as I watch him go. "Nice arse!" I note. "Am I permitted to say that on our first date?"

He giggles and attempts to cover his arse with his splayed hand. "No, you are not!" He plonks his sexy arse back in his seat and rings the bell for the main course to be served. The waiter suddenly appears as if from nowhere, like a spirit summoned, and clears our bowls away.

The rest of the dinner date flies by. I discover Aiden is actually quite the flirt; it's just kinky talk he shies away from. I make mental notes as I go. This is all potentially useful information. I want Aiden to like me so he keeps inviting me back.

Too soon I find myself slumped in the back of the taxicab with a familiar jazz track playing on the radio. I'm glad I pre-booked a room in a little hotel on the coast. I'd hate to have to start searching for a hotel with vacancies at this time of night. No doubt when a young lady attends for a dinner date, she's offered a bed for the night at Foxwell Manor, but there was never any danger of Lord Foxwell agreeing to me staying under his roof. Still, at least Aiden has invited me back tomorrow for a personal tour of the gardens, so all-in-all it's been a very successful first contact.

During the twenty-minute drive to the hotel I find myself rehashing the events of the evening in my mind. A spontaneous grin breaks out across my face and I can't help wondering why I'm feeling so high. I've never felt this way after a dinner date before, so what was it about my visit to Foxwell Manor that's left me in this oddly euphoric state? I've dined at lots of fancy restaurants and tasted the finest wines, so none of that is new to me, therefore I can only conclude it must have been Aiden's delightful company. I have to admit, as surprising as it is, I *did* find him hugely entertaining and I don't remember the last time I thought that about anyone. It's nice to be able to combine business with pleasure. I expect I'll have to spend several days, if not weeks, here in the middle of nowhere, biding my time until I get a chance to scrutinise the painting, so it's nice that Aiden is such a pleasing distraction. It will make the time pass much faster and I'm already looking forward to my return visit.

12 – AIDEN

I jump into bed, my belly full, my mind a little groggy from the wine. There's a smile fixed to my lips and I just can't seem to shift it. I'm not sure what it is about Mackenzie Oden, but there were definite sparks of chemistry between us this evening, which I totally wasn't expecting. He appeals to me on a visceral level and I always think your initial gut reaction to someone is worth taking note of.

I'll admit he's not your typical tall, dark and handsome. In fact, you could argue he isn't any of those things. He has a decent enough body, but he's not particularly tall and his hair is fair, not dark. Is he handsome? Well, not if you apply traditional standards of measurement. His eyes are set too deep, his nose is too sharp and pointy, and his face too long, but somehow the whole ensemble works for me. He sports a closely-shaved beard that I'm oddly excited about. I've never been kissed by a man with facial hair before and I find it a tantalising prospect.

Bottom line is I can't wait to see Mackenzie again and discover what his intentions are with regard to me. Any man who can stand up to my dad has my respect. But more than that, Mackenzie is an enigma and I want to know what makes him tick. I get the impression he's a bit of a chameleon, fitting in whether he's in good company or bad. Yes, he can be brazen and brusque, but I like that about him. He's the sort of man who's capable of getting me into all kinds of trouble, and trouble is exactly what I'm looking for to spice up my life.

13 – MACKENZIE

Truth be told, I was glad I didn't get an invite to stay at Foxwell Manor last night. I wouldn't have slept very well after the heated exchange of words with Lord Foxwell. I'd have had one eye open all night, expecting the shadow of an axeman to appear in my doorway. Nevertheless, I'm glad to be back again today, after Aiden offered to give me a personal tour of the gardens. Of course, I'd much rather be having a tour of the house so I can check out their security system and maybe even get my first glimpse of the painting, but that'll have to wait.

Aiden and I enjoy a light lunch of sandwiches and cake before taking our stroll outside, away from the prying eyes and ears of Lord Foxwell. We head past the fountain, through a gap in the hedge, to a track alongside a bed of multi-coloured dahlias. The track leads to a walled kitchen garden, where neat rows of red cabbage, beetroot and purple-sprouting broccoli sit alongside trellised runner beans coming to the end of their season. We walk around the grassy edge to the far side, to where a wrought iron gate leads out onto a slightly raised area of land. There's a wooden seat waiting for us there and I notice that on its curved back there's a brass plaque, dedicated to the loving memory of Lady Alice Foxwell. Aiden invites me to sit.

From our slightly elevated position, we can see the layout of all the formal gardens as they follow the seemingly never-ending line of trees down the driveway to the distant high brick wall that surrounds the entire estate. In addition to this spot being south-facing, the walled garden behind us provides shelter from the swirling autumn breeze.

"This was my mum's favourite spot," Aiden notes.

"I can see why," I concur. "Great views and a perfect suntrap."

Aiden is dressed in casuals today, wearing dove-grey jeans and a black t-shirt. He sits perched on the edge of the seat, his back arrow straight, hands resting on his knees, probably in the manner he was taught to sit when his mother was alive.

"I hardly ever come here anymore," Aiden says, staring straight ahead in an almost trance-like state.

"Why?"

"Too many memories. I used to come here with my mum whenever either of us needed a break from my dad. She'd nod towards the door and I knew what she meant. We'd meet up here and just talk. After she died, it made me feel sad coming here on my own so I stopped."

"Has your father always been a domineering ogre?"

Aiden gives a good-natured huff. "Honestly, he's not that bad. Don't judge him on the confrontation you had with him last night. He probably just thought he was protecting me. He doesn't know you from Adam, and you have to admit that bidding on an auction isn't a conventional way to get to know someone, if that's what this is about." He pauses as if he's waiting for me to respond, but I say nothing so he continues. "Dad has old-fashioned views about him being the head of the family, and about duty and responsibility. He needs to learn to chill, that's all." He turns to face me. "Why aren't you married?"

"Sorry?" I gasp, taken aback by the abrupt change of subject.

"Frankie, our head of security, copied your notes to me, but I only gave them a cursory scan. I was fuming with you at the time and had little interest in getting to know you better, but two things stood out for me. You're not married and your mum died when you were young. We have that in common at least. Has your dad remarried, or is he too busy chasing skirt, like mine?"

"My dad died ten years ago. Heart attack."

"Oh, sorry!" His shoulders slump and he shifts his position so he's leaning against the back of the seat, as if he's suddenly realised no-one is watching and he can relax. "To be fair to my dad, he's not chasing skirt anymore. He seems to have settled on one, for the time being. She's only about ten years older than me but she's nice. Her name is Hannah Reece."

"I believe I saw her at the auction."

"Oh yes, that's right. She's quite a sporty type so she's keeping my dad fit, which can't be a bad thing at his age. You might get to meet her later. She's gone into Peterborough to do a bit of shopping. They're planning a big trip abroad. I think they decided on Canada in the end."

"Are you not invited?"

He snorts. "As if I'd want to play gooseberry."

"What will you do while they're gone?"

He shrugs. "Nothing much. I don't see that much of my dad on a day-to-day basis anyway, so I won't really miss him. He's long since abdicated any responsibility for me. He gave Frankie that onerous task not long after my mum died. Anyway, you didn't answer my question."

"What was that?"

"Why aren't you married?"

"Why should I be?"

"I would hope I am by the time I'm…"

"By the time you're what? My age?"

"I just meant that you're…you know."

"No. What?"

"You're not bad looking."

"Is that the same as good looking?"

Aiden chuckles. "Not quite, but I'm surprised you're still on the shelf."

"On the shelf? What am I, some out-of-date fig roll?"

"Don't you want to get married?"

"It's never entered my mind. Why? Are you offering?"

He ignores my quip. "Do you have a boyfriend?"

I smirk at him. "Why don't you check your notes?"

"I deleted them. Besides, they only told me your marital status. I'm asking about your love life. Just because you're single, doesn't mean you're not dating."

"Did you say *love* life? Sorry, I'm not familiar

with that term. I have a sex life."

"Oh, I see. You're one of those types, are you? A quick wham-bam and then move on to the next."

Of course I could lie to him, tell him I'm a hearts-and-flowers type of guy, but anyone who spends more than five minutes with me would know that's not true. Besides I'm so confident of my ability to seduce young Foxwell that I can't be bothered to lie. He's going to succumb to my charms anyway. They always do. In fact, he'll probably want me more if I tell him I'm a hard-nosed bastard. I don't know why, but apparently that presents some kind of challenge. I'm a bit like Mount Everest. There are unimaginable obstacles in the way of ever conquering my heart but that doesn't stop an endless flow of foolhardy optimists thinking they're the one to do it.

"I'm not going to lie to you, Aiden. I enjoy sex and I've never felt the need to limit my opportunities, not even by gender."

"Oh!" He stares at me for a moment. "So you're into men *and* women?"

I shrug. "What's the point in limiting yourself to half the population?"

"You think a choice of 30 million people is limiting?"

I gaze into his eyes. "Well, right now I'm only interested in one."

"In your dreams, Mackenzie. When I have sex with someone it has to mean something."

"It generally means a damn good time as far as I'm concerned."

"Yeah, I bet you steal hearts everywhere you go and then dump them by text."

I tilt my head back and eye him down the barrel of my nose. "You're assuming that I bother to ask for their phone number."

Aiden grunts. "You're a real charmer. It's actually becoming quite clear to me now why you're still single."

"Well, maybe I just haven't met the right person yet. How about you?" I ask. "Anyone serious in your life? Boyfriend? Girlfriend?"

He shakes his head. "I'm gay. Why would I have a girlfriend?"

"Well, you auction yourself off for a dinner date with the ladies and I imagine, after a drink or two, she expects at least a kiss. Are you telling me you've never gone there?"

"No. The auction is my dad's idea, not mine. I play along but strictly to the letter. It's a dinner date, that's all. He wants me to pretend I'm straight until I've given him a grandchild, but I hate it. It's deceitful."

"So why don't you tell him that's how you feel?"

"I have. I told him that my sexual orientation isn't negotiable, nor does it come with a get-out clause for the purposes of procreation."

"Good for you. And what did he say to that?"

"He lectured me on my duty to continue the family line and reminded me how privileged I am." Aiden gets to his feet. "Come on. Let's get out of here."

"And go where?"

"For a drive."

We retrace our steps through the walled garden and as we pass the dahlias, Aiden picks up again where the conversation left off.

"That's the thing about being a Foxwell. You have to produce an heir otherwise you're letting down your ancestors. It's all about the accumulation of wealth and property and keeping it in the family. It *always* comes back to money. Sometimes I wish I could break away and stand on my own two feet. I've lived my entire life behind these walls, security guards watching my every move, catching me when I fall. I'm sick of being wrapped in cotton wool."

We reach the fountain in front of the main entrance and I notice Aiden's car is now parked outside the front door, the roof already stowed, and I presume he must have arranged in advance for someone to get it out of the garage for him.

I grip Aiden's upper arm and twist him around to face me. Confronted by his big brown eyes, I feel an excited tingle spreading south from my gut to regions I don't even want to think about right now.

"What's stopping you leaving this place?"

"Money. It *always* comes back to money."

"You're kidding. You must be loaded." I nod towards the car. "What about the DB11?"

"Please! It's not a DB11. It's a DB11 Volante. I wouldn't be caught dead in a coupé."

"Begging your pardon, Your Lordship," I tease, glancing down at his plump red lips, so close to mine.

"Anyway, my dad paid for the car. It's him that's loaded, not me. He's not stupid enough to give me access to the purse strings or he'd never see me for dust. He gives me an allowance—just enough to keep me ticking over. Oh, and our credit is good at the local garage so I can fill up whenever I want. Other than that, I'm totally reliant on him."

"Reliant. On your father," I repeat dryly. "Well, here's a novel concept for you, Aiden. Why not get yourself a job? Just a thought."

He grunts. "You expect me to slum it at a nine-to-five?"

"I'm sure it'd do you the world of good to build up an honest sweat."

Aiden moves a step closer and looks me right in the eyes. "I'm a gentleman. Gentlemen don't sweat."

"Oh, I'm pretty sure I could make you sweat, Aiden Foxwell," I say in a throaty growl. His eyes drop to my mouth and it's all the encouragement I need. I pull him to me and claim those pouty lips of his. At first he responds, his pliable mouth moving eagerly against mine, lips parting so I can feel the warmth of his breath, but then he pulls away and, without warning, he slaps my face.

"What was that for?" I yelp.

"Your beard tickles."

"You slapped me because my beard tickles?"

"And my dad might be watching."

Aiden sets off towards the front door, leaving me to follow behind, still dazed by his bewildering reaction. Once we're inside, Aiden hands me my leather jacket from the coat stand.

"Am I leaving?"

"We both are. I told you, we're going for a drive. I just need to grab a few things from upstairs. Wait here. I'll be back in a jiffy."

14 – AIDEN

He's acting like he's really into me. Of course I'm used to that. Someone in my position gets a lot of attention from people who pretend to be interested when it's actually my family's wealth they're attracted to. I know how to separate the wheat from the chaff though. Play hard to get. Give them reasons to think I'm too much effort. Only if they genuinely like me will they persist.

Mackenzie's attitude to relationships suggests he gets bored easily, so let's see how long he hangs around without getting any kind of pay-off. He probably has a thing for rich kids and just wants me to be another notch on his headboard.

Thing is, I *do* really like him. He's easy to chat to and he stands up to my dad. These are very desirable qualities as far as I'm concerned. He has what I call "compatibility potential" so I'm hoping he'll stick around long enough for me to figure out if he's for real. If he is, and if he's patient with me, I think he'll find I'm worth the wait.

15 – MACKENZIE

I shrug my leather jacket on as I wait in the hallway for Aiden. My mind keeps replaying the brief kiss and the slap that followed. Aiden's an odd creature. I'm finding it hard to get a handle on how he's really feeling about me.

I hear footsteps coming down the stairs and turn to see Aiden now has a light sweater draped over his shoulders, but it's what's on his face that makes my jaw drop. His eyes are hidden behind a pair of hideous reflective sunglasses with rainbow-striped lenses. My lip curls without even waiting for a signal from my brain.

"Come on, let's get going," Aiden says as he breezes past me, grabbing his car key off the side table as he heads for the door.

"You go ahead," I insist. "I think I'll walk a few paces behind."

"They usually do," he quips as he flings the front door open and sashays across the drive towards his garishly-orange car. "But you're still expected to hold the car door open for me."

Cheeky runt! "I'm not a member of your bloody staff," I call out as I follow him.

"Chill, Mackenzie. It was a joke." Aiden points his remote key at the DB11 and it flashes all its lights at him, as if it's the paparazzi and he's on the red carpet. He slips into the driver's side and slams the door shut.

I open the passenger door and feast my eyes on the sumptuously-fitted cockpit. I'm very pleased to note Aiden opted for a more demure colour scheme for the interior. The black leather seats have only the merest hint of orange in the brogueing. I slide in and close the door.

"Um…you do know how to drive this thing, don't you? I mean without slamming into a tree or anything."

Aiden gives me a quirky look. "Who's been talking?"

"No-one," I lie. "I noticed a damaged tree up the drive."

"Nothing to do with me," Aiden insists.

"Bullshit," I say on a cough.

"Sorry?"

"Where are we going?" I enquire timorously.

"To the coast. That's where you said you're staying, isn't it? I thought I'd drive you back to your hotel, save you ordering another taxi."

"Oh, how kind," I say with a fake smile.

"Hi, Frankie!" Aiden calls out to a gent in a work suit who's just come from one of the outbuildings. I recognise the name as Aiden mentioned him while we were in the garden. He's their head of security, if I recall correctly. "Just popping out for a drive," Aiden tells him. "I'll be back by teatime."

"Very good, sir." Frankie says and heads towards the house, pausing at the front door. "Oh, and sir," he calls out, twisting around to face us.

"Don't say it, Frankie," Aiden warns.

"Drive carefully, sir."

Aiden squeals like a pig and Frankie chuckles softly to himself as he disappears inside.

"I hate it when he says that," Aiden complains.

I laugh nervously, worried that Frankie has good reason to caution Aiden about his driving, but equally concerned that Frankie's comment might have antagonised Aiden just as we're about to set off. I know when I was young, if someone cautioned me in a nagging kind of way, I'd usually do the exact thing they didn't want me to do, just to spite them. My body flips into panic mode, releasing a surge of adrenalin that floods my bloodstream and sets my heart racing.

Aiden presses the start button in the centre of the dash causing the engine to rev to 2200 RPM with an accompanying growl. I grope around the edge of my seat, searching for the ejector button, just in case. The engine quickly drops back to idle, settling into a rumbling purr as it waits politely for Aiden's next command.

Aiden turns to me, his eyes hidden behind those hideous lenses. He grins at me, baring a row of blindingly-white piano-key teeth. "Buckle up, Mackenzie. This little baby is Jessica and she's dying to show you what *0-60 in 4 seconds* feels like."

"Oh fuck!" I whimper as I fumble for my seatbelt. I've barely strapped myself in before Aiden's foot hits the floor. We shoot off up the drive like a twin-turbocharged cheetah, my jaw clenched with fear as the force of the torque buries me deep in my seat.

My God, my life is in the hands of a twenty-two-year-old! I might not live long enough to clap eyes on the bloody painting.

A few nanoseconds later we're spat out onto the public road, or rather the narrow country lane that passes for a road around Foxwell Manor. Aiden turns on the local radio, pumping the volume up so we can hear it above the roar of the engine and the wind rushing past our ears. Ed Sheeran's "Castle On The Hill" is playing and its energetic vibe is the perfect accompaniment as we set off on our wild ride to the coast.

By some miracle, we survive the journey and it's not long before we're slowing to a leisurely crawl as we enter the village of Old Hunstanton, where Aiden pulls into a car park and cuts the engine.

"I'm not actually staying here," I inform him. "I'm staying down the road in Hunstanton."

Aiden turns to face me and smirks. "You sound like a tourist. We pronounce it 'Hunston' around these parts."

"I *am* a tourist, and please lose those ridiculous sunglasses. You look like a camp version of The Terminator."

"Come with me if you want to live," Aiden says in a robotic Austrian accent, sounding exactly like Schwarzenegger.

I can't help but laugh. "Wow! That was like having Arnie sat right next to me."

"Hasta la vista, baby."

"Yeah, okay," I say holding my hands up in surrender. "Enough already. Why are we here when my hotel is a mile down the road?"

Aiden pulls the sunglasses off and tosses them on the backseat. "I thought we'd walk the rest of the way. We can do the Wolf Trail and then take a stroll along the beach to your hotel."

"Aww, how romantic!" I sneer.

The Wolf Trail, it turns out, is a pleasant stroll along a grassy cliff top and includes a magnificent solid oak carving of a howling wolf, which Aiden can't wait to tell me about.

"This is to celebrate the life of Edmund the Martyr. He was the first patron saint of England, an Anglo-Saxon king who was killed by Viking invaders when he wasn't much older than me. Apparently he was tied to a tree and they used him as target practice until he had so many arrows sticking out of him he looked like a porcupine."

"Ouch!"

"Yeah. And then for good measure they chopped off his head and threw it in the forest. And that's where the wolf comes in. It made sure the forest predators didn't eat the head so it could be reunited with the body, so the wolf is kind of the hero of the piece."

I pat the wolf on the head. "Good for you!"

After completing the trail we take a leisurely stroll along the shoreline, heading towards the far end of the resort where my hotel is located. It's getting near the end of the season so the beach isn't overly crowded, especially as the sea breeze has turned a bit chilly. Aiden slips his sweater on and links arms with me. Considering the slap to the face my kiss engendered, I'm surprised at this display of affection now that we're away from Foxwell Manor. Not that I'm complaining. I feel honoured to have this sexy and sophisticated young man on my arm. Of course, it would be a whole other story if he hadn't ditched the sunglasses.

"This is me," I say finally, nodding towards the

hotel across the road from the beach. I turn to face him, wrapping my arms around his waist to pull him in close. "Are you coming in for coffee?"

Aiden gazes at me as if he's considering it.

"Your father's not watching now, is he?" I say, hoping to make up his mind for him.

"It's not that."

"Then what?"

Aiden responds with a kiss—a kiss so sweet and tender you might almost describe it as respectfully staid. When we separate I scan his face, trying to figure him out.

"Why are you looking at me like that?"

"I'm waiting for the slap."

He chuckles. "Relax, Mackenzie, you're safe."

"Beard not too ticklish?"

"No, I like the way it feels."

"Aren't you worried about setting people's tongues wagging, holding hands and kissing in public?"

"Do you know what, Mackenzie? I'm tired of playing by my dad's rules. I'm old enough to make up my own rules now. You won't find me selling my integrity to the highest bidder at next year's auction.

"Good for you. So, are you coming back to my room or not?"

"No."

"Why not?"

"I don't want to be just another notch on your headboard, Mackenzie."

"I'd burn the bloody headboard for you."

He looks at me curiously. "Are you serious?"

I snort. "No. I don't even have a headboard. It's a brass bed. All the better to tie you to."

"Don't get any weird ideas. I'm not into kink. I'm just a regular boy looking for love."

"There's nothing regular about you, Aiden Foxwell, and it's never wise to go looking for love. Love isn't something that's there for the taking. It grows from something else. Maybe something as wild and crazy as a fling with a stranger."

"Do they usually fall for that line and jump straight into the sack with you after you've uttered your words of wisdom."

"You're very cynical for one so young."

"I think I need to be on my guard with you, Mackenzie."

"Why? Are you worried you're getting to like me too much?"

Aiden gives me a coy smile. "Come see me again tomorrow?"

"If you'd like me to."

"I would."

I nod and then it occurs to me that there's a chance to promote my agenda. "You've shown me around the gardens, so how about giving me a tour of the house next time?"

"Okay. Same time?"

I nod and then he pulls free of my arms as he spots a taxicab coming towards us. He runs over to the path to hail it and the cab pulls over.

"What about your car?" I shout after him.

"You don't think I'm walking all the way back to the car park, do you?"

He ducks into the taxi and then he's gone.

As I head back to my hotel, I feel a twinge of excitement in my gut. With any luck, tomorrow I'll finally set eyes on the painting.

16 – AIDEN

Despite Mackenzie asking for a tour of the house, he doesn't seem particularly interested in any of the rooms I show him, even though I'm doing my very best impression of a tour guide.

"This is the piano I attempted to play as a kid. My mum tried her best to teach me, but I have no musical talent whatsoever. Even my dog used to cover his ears."

Mackenzie seems distracted. He's glancing around the room, gazing at the walls, completely ignoring me.

I fold my arms and glare at the side of his face. "Am I boring you?"

He jerks his head back around to face me. "I thought these grand old houses were full of antiques and old masters."

I huff. "Sorry to disappoint you, Mackenzie, but you can blame my grandparents for selling off most of the original antiques. They needed the money to pay for the upkeep of the house. The Foxwells were asset rich and cash poor until my mum married into the family. She was the one with all the money. She loved collecting antiques so she'd started adding pieces here and there, but my dad has auctioned most of those off now too."

"And you have no artwork either?"

"Oh sure. We have some paintings. That's the one thing my grandparents didn't sell. My dad's added a few to the collection recently too. I don't know why. I never thought he was really that interested in art. I think he just likes to have nice pieces on the wall so he can show off to his friends at Christmas."

"I'm an art lover. Would you mind if I take a look at your collection?"

I hesitate for a moment. "I think it'll be okay. Dad and Hannah are playing golf today."

"Why does it matter where your father is?"

"He doesn't like me taking people upstairs. And when I say people I mean men, of course. He'd be over the moon if I took a girl upstairs."

"Oh, I see. The artwork is upstairs. Well, I don't want to get you into trouble, so maybe just a quick peek?"

"Okay, just a quickie. Come with me." I grab Mackenzie's hand and lead him out into the grand hall and then we run up the stairs together like a couple of excited kids, sneaking off to do something naughty. When we reach the landing at the top, I have a fleeting thought of turning right and taking Mackenzie to my room, but I quickly dismiss such a ludicrous urge. I turn left and then halt so he can take it all in. "Welcome to our little home gallery? What do you think?"

"Oh my God!" Mackenzie drawls, letting go of my hand. I stand and watch as he makes a beeline for the latest addition to the collection— the one my dad acquired on the black market.

I suddenly recall the day my dad warned me to be wary of Mackenzie. His words start floating in and out of my mind, repeating on me like a bad case of heartburn.

"You need to be on your guard when there are

100

strangers in the house. The last painting I acquired cost me an awful lot of money."

"If he's a thief, he's hardly going to include that in his bloody résumé, is he?

"This complete stranger has coughed up ten grand to gain access to the house. It strikes me as extremely odd."

It's very telling that Mackenzie went straight to that painting without giving any of the others a second glance. It's as if he knew what he was looking for. It's clear now that it's the painting he wanted to see when he asked for a tour of the house. He wasn't interested in anything else I had to show him. That's why he was so distracted downstairs. He was looking for this. He specifically asked if he could see the artwork.

I've been such an idiot.

I don't know what to do. I've shown it to him now. I can't *un-show* it to him. But maybe I can tease some information out of Mackenzie and find out just how much he actually knows about this painting.

17 – MACKENZIE

At the top of the solid oak staircase is a spectacular galleried landing. It's basically an open parapet on one side with a wooden balustrade and columns—a bit like the Grand Circle in an old theatre, except that all along the back wall is a row of magnificent artwork.

"Welcome to our little home gallery? What do you think?" Aiden says proudly.

I quickly scan the paintings with the gleeful awe of a kid in a sweetshop and even amid such prestigious company, it doesn't take me long to spot what appears to be a Raphael.

I gasp. "Oh my God!"

I walk forward on shaky legs, my head buzzing, heart pounding, and after ten paces I'm standing directly in front of it. Aiden follows me, standing beside me as we gaze up at the portrait.

"This is…it's…wow!" I'm not normally lost for words in the presence of a great work of art. Usually you can't shut me up. "It must be a fake."

"Sorry? What do you know about this painting?" Aiden asks.

"It's unbelievable," I mutter.

"It's unsigned," he points out.

"You'd be surprised how many old masters are unsigned. Many artists considered it an uncouth act of self-promotion to sign pieces, especially ones they'd been commissioned to produce. If they could have envisaged the sort of life humans would end up living, in a world dominated by social media and advertising, it would have been a total anathema to them."

"So you're saying this is an old master?"

"It certainly looks that way at first glance." I turn to face Aiden. "Where did your father get this painting?"

Aiden blanches. "I don't know. Don't you want to look at the others?"

"Everything else is going to pale into insignificance next to this."

"What did you say you do for a living?" Aiden asks tentatively.

"Art historian." Well, it's not exactly a lie. I do the odd bit of legit work on the side, just for the sake of appearances.

"So you work in a gallery?"

"No. I'm more of a private gun for hire. I get called in by wealthy collectors when there's an art-related issue they need me to resolve."

"So if, for example, there was a certain piece someone wanted to acquire, you'd be the man to get it for them."

Aiden and I exchange a long silent stare. I'm not sure how this conversation switched around to me rather than the painting, but we're getting on dodgy ground now. Aiden's suggestion that I can get a client whatever painting they want is a bit odd. Clearly, a painting can only be legally purchased if and when the current owner decides to sell. People tend to hang onto art. The more valuable a piece, the less likely it is to change hands on a regular basis.

"It's true that if an item comes up for sale I may be asked to attend the auction and bid on behalf of the client, but actually an art historian's job is mostly cataloguing. For instance, I might get called in when someone dies and the paintings are inherited by the next generation. Family members rarely have a clue about the artwork on their walls, so they ask me to catalogue it and advise them how much it's worth."

Aiden nods towards the painting. "So how much is this one worth?"

I follow his gaze and give a wry smile. "That depends on whether its authenticity can be established. If this is what it appears to be, it's worth a jaw-dropping sum."

Aiden huffs. "I'd refuse to pay you if that was your best guess at a valuation. Where did you learn about art, at a paint-by-numbers class? I suppose anyone can call themselves an art historian. It's not like you need a licence to prove it."

I slowly turn to face him, wondering why he felt the need to make such a snide remark. If there's one thing that really pushes my nose out of joint it's someone questioning my expertise. I consider myself one of the country's foremost art experts. Whether I choose to use my knowledge for legal or illegal gains is between me and my conscience. I'm still at the top of my game, whether I'm legit or a thief, but if young Foxwell needs a lecture in how to value artwork, I'm happy to educate the cheeky little runt.

"Let me put it this way," I say stiff-jawed. "Aside from not having seen a certificate of provenance for this painting, there are three other major obstacles to accurately valuing it. The first obstacle is the time lag. The last time this painting legally changed hands was over 200 years ago. I say 'legally' because I'm assuming your father obtained this on the black market, otherwise the sale of such a rare piece would most certainly have hit the headlines. But we'll come back to that in a moment. The point I'm trying to make is that any piece of art that so rarely comes to market is going to be virtually impossible to value with any real conviction. The very fact it is notoriously hard to acquire makes bidding patterns insanely unpredictable. Are you following me so far?"

Aiden nods, his eyes wide as if he's taken aback by my rant.

"The second obstacle to providing an accurate valuation is the artist himself. You see, Raphael's work never comes to market, so if one did, it would cause an almighty feeding frenzy. We're talking silly money. You can't put a valuation on 'silly.' It's just a number with lots of zeros after it."

"You think it's a Raphael?" Aiden asks, his face a sickly grey.

"It certainly looks that way and the thing is, Aiden, there aren't supposed to be any of his in private collections. Well, that's not strictly true. There are a number of Raphael's in the Royal Collection, but they're never going to come to market. Likewise, the Duke of Sutherland has a couple on semi-permanent loan to a gallery. Basically, there is zero chance of a private collector legally obtaining a Raphael. So, we return to the fact that your father must have acquired his on the black market. But this isn't

106

any old Raphael. This is a very special Raphael, and that leads me neatly to the third obstacle in the way of accurately valuing this piece. This painting is supposed to be missing."

Aiden gulps. "What do you mean?"

"It was supposed to have been a casualty of war. It was snatched by the Nazis during the Second World War and it hasn't been seen since. Historians have long thought it was among a vast collection lost in a fire at the end of the war, but every now and then rumours have surfaced of it being hidden in a bank vault somewhere in Europe. If this is the genuine article, then those rumours were true, and it has since been released from the vault and changed hands on the black market. So, Aiden, it would appear your father has connections to the underworld."

A smirk stretches across my face as I realise that Lord Foxwell and I really aren't so very different after all. "In fact," I declare triumphantly, "it's fair to say your father is no better than a thief. *No better at all.*"

18 – AIDEN

I'm such a fool. I should have listened to my dad. I can't believe it. Is this whole thing really a set-up? Has Mackenzie been playing me all along? Did he only bid on that auction so he could use me to gain access to the painting?

I feel so sick. I was just starting to like him too. I mean *really* like him. How can this be happening to me? Finally I meet someone I like but all he's interested in is that stupid painting. And the way he ranted on about it and accused my dad of being no better than him.

My dad! No better than a thief! How dare you say that, Mackenzie Oden?

Well, if this is how you want it, two can play games, and then we'll see which of us is the better player. I suppose you think I'm just some dumb kid you can walk all over, but I'm really not, and I'm about to prove it to you.

You've just bitten off way more than you can chew, Mr. Oden.

19 – MACKENZIE

It's a miserable day in Hunstanton. High winds batter hard pellets of rain against the sash window of my hotel room, leaving long streaks that blur the sea-view upgrade I paid for.

It's been two days since I finally got to view the painting and I'm still trying to get my head around the magnitude of this find, if it is indeed genuine. I need to study it in more detail, but the five minutes viewing time Aiden gave me still proved to be a useful exercise. I noticed there were two I.D. scanners—one either side of the painting—so Lord Foxwell has a state-of-the-art security system installed. That's going to make life very difficult for me, maybe even impossible, but I'll need to get a closer look at that too before I can make a final judgement.

I'm still waiting for another invite back to Foxwell Manor. Aiden didn't make any arrangements for us to meet up again at the end of my last visit, but I'm not going anywhere anytime soon. I booked the hotel room for a couple of weeks initially, but I'll carry on extending my stay as long as it takes. Hopefully it won't be too long before I get another invite back. I told Aiden I've decided to take a break off work to stay on the coast for a couple of weeks, so he knows I'm available to meet up.

In the meantime, I've been researching the chequered history of the painting. Raphael created the portrait in 1514, just a few years after his contemporary, Da Vinci, painted the

Mona Lisa. The same angled pose has been adopted—known as the three-quarter view—and typically there is a scenic view in the background. Raphael's earlier works, *Young Man in Red* and *Young Woman With Unicorn* both utilised this traditional pose, as had other Renaissance artists, such as Francesca del Cossa and Marco Basaiti.

Although it started life in Rome, by the end of the eighteenth century it had been purchased by a Polish prince to display in the Czartoryski Museum in Kraków. This was not a good move for the painting. Poland was at the epicentre of a Europe in turmoil. Nations were land-grabbing and rulers were being toppled. Poland had once been the second largest European state until it was carved up by its neighbours. It seemed there was always a war being waged somewhere on the continent. The French Revolution, the Napoleonic Wars, the Franco-Prussian War, all followed by a seemingly never-ending spate of battles, invasions and uprisings that finally culminated in two world wars. As a result, the painting spent much of its life hidden away to avoid being looted by invading forces. Unfortunately, it was finally discovered during the Second World War, becoming one of the innumerable works of art plundered by the Nazis.

As I gaze at an online image of the painting my phone pings.

It's a message from Aiden.

Aiden: *If you're available tomorrow afternoon I can pick you up at two. You can have a longer look at the painting if you want. Dad and Hannah* *have gone to Canada.*

That sounds like the perfect way for me to spend an afternoon, so I quickly tap in my response.

Mackenzie: *Sounds great. No need to pick me up. I'll grab a taxi.*

My phone pings again two seconds later.

Aiden: *Bring an overnight bag.*

An overnight bag! Well, there's a turn up for the books. I suppose now that his daddy is away Aiden has decided to play. Lucky me!

20 – AIDEN

I watch Mackenzie as he stares intently at the painting, his eyes scanning it inch by inch. I know what he is now—a thief. I also know what this painting is—a masterpiece. I quizzed my dad about it before he left for Canada. I now know why he purchased it, and that he paid hush money to an independent expert to verify its authenticity. I don't approve of the way my dad has been spending my inheritance. Both he and Mackenzie have fucked me over in favour of this painting. That's a hard thing to forgive. All I can do now is try to flip this whole scenario on its head and somehow manufacture myself a positive outcome. It's all I've been thinking about these past two days.

"So, what do you think? Is it genuine or not? My dad had it independently checked, but as you appear to have some knowledge in these matters, I was hoping for a second opinion."

"Well, it has all the right attributes."

"What attributes are those?"

"It *looks* like a Raphael. You get an eye for these things. I can usually spot a fake a mile off. If this is a fake it's extremely well done."

"Anything else?"

"It definitely appears to have a lot of age to it. It's oil on wood—probably either poplar or linden for the wooden panel, with walnut oil as the mixing medium. The frame isn't original, but that's a positive as far as I'm concerned. You don't go to the trouble of creating a copy only to put the wrong frame on it. I can't really say much more than that while it's still hung. I'd need to give it a closer inspection." Mackenzie switches his gaze to me. "Isn't your father worried about having a stolen masterpiece hung on his wall for all to see? I'd be afraid of getting arrested."

I snort. "I expect that's an occupational hazard for you."

Mackenzie scowls at me. "Sorry?"

I clamour for an excuse for my little dig. "I mean having to determine if a painting is genuine or not. You must get bored of getting asked that." Biting my tongue has always been problematic for me, so I suspect my little dig about getting arrested is going to be the first of many to fall from my lips today.

"But don't you agree it's risky? Your father is in possession of stolen goods."

"He didn't steal it. He paid a lot of money for it."

"But whoever he purchased it from had no legal claim to it in the first place. Personally, I'd have it out of sight, in a safety deposit box."

"You're right, but my dad has friends in high places and that tends to make a man foolishly brave. He imagines he's untouchable. And of course, not many people would even know what it is, other than some random unsigned painting of a man. There's nothing spectacular about it to make it instantly recognisable. I'm not even sure I really like it. It's a bit...boring."

"Boring!" Mackenzie scoffs. "It's a bloody portrait, not the Battle of Waterloo. What do you want to see, fireworks coming out of his ears?"

"Who is it supposed to be of?"

"No-one knows for certain, but it's believed to be a self-portrait of the young Raphael himself."

"Really?" I say, peering more closely at the painting. "And what title did he give to this jaw-droppingly valuable self-portrait?"

"*Portrait of a Young Man.*"

"Oh!" I groan, turning to look at Mackenzie. "That's not very original, is it? He really needed a marketing guru to come up with something better than that. I'd have called it *Me Before I Was Famous.*"

Mackenzie laughs. "Except he was getting commissions from the pope by the time he painted this, so I think he was already guaranteed eternal fame by then."

"Imagine that!" I sigh. "Eternal fame. He doesn't look much older than me. I wish I had a talent for something. I've always felt like a piece of useless driftwood, being dragged back and forth by the tides of time, with no real purpose in life."

Mackenzie huffs. "You'll figure it out eventually. We all have a talent for something. It just takes some people a lot longer to work out what it is. My neighbour was fifty when he got made redundant from a job he hated and then, when he suddenly found himself with loads of free time on his hands, he discovered he had a talent for drawing. He's now working as a magazine illustrator and loving every second of it."

"That's depressing," I complain. "I don't want to wait until I'm fifty to find out what I'm good at."

"That was just an example. You might discover your talent next week, next month, next year. Who knows?"

"Would you like to examine it more closely?" I ask nonchalantly.

Mackenzie's eyes lock onto mine. "Examine what?"

"The painting, of course. I can get it down for you."

He gawks at me in slack-jawed silence.

Mackenzie's face is priceless. I've never felt such a rush of power as I do at this precise moment. Mackenzie thinks he's running this show, but it's actually *me* who's getting a kick out of toying with *him*. Look at him! He can hardly contain himself. He looks ready to get on the floor and kiss my feet. I can't wait to see his face when he figures out that I'm onto him.

"I'll take that as a yes," I say. "I just need to call our head of security. Hang on a second." I move back along the corridor to where there's an intercom on the wall. I slam the button with the side of my fist to open communications and speak into the microphone. "Frankie, it's me. I'm on the gallery landing. Need your assistance."

"On my way, sir," comes the immediate response.

A couple of paces beyond the intercom there's a table with a drawer underneath it from where I grab a pair of gloves, ready to hand to Frankie. The sound of heavy footsteps running up the creaking wooden staircase heralds Frankie's arrival. Breathless and panicked, his gaze flicks between me and Mackenzie. "Is there a problem, sir?"

"No problem," I say with a saccharine smile. "I'd just like to take a closer look at that one." I point at the Raphael.

Frankie looks like he's about to faint. "A closer look?" he repeats, his voice a high-pitched squeak.

"That's right," I reply casually.

"I'll get a ladder and a magnifying glass," Frankie says turning to leave.

"No," I reply emphatically, halting him in his tracks. "I want you to help me with the alarm."

I watch the power dynamic between young Aiden and his stockily-built middle-aged security chief. Frankie's turned as white as a ghost and the deep frown lines etched in his face are, no doubt, the result of years of service, attempting to keep Aiden in line and out of trouble, despite having no real authority over the boy.

"Shouldn't you wait for your father to get back from Canada?" Frankie suggests.

"And what was the point of setting you up with authorisation if I have to wait for him to return from wherever he happens to be? What do you think I'm going to do, run off with it?" Aiden nods towards me. "Mr. Oden is an art historian and he'd like to study the painting in more detail. I've already said that he can. You may wait at the bottom of the stairs until we're finished, if it makes you feel better."

That last sentence brooked no argument and Frankie sighs wearily, knowing he's defeated. "Very good, sir."

I watch intently, making a mental note of every move as Aiden and Frankie position themselves either side of the painting, each lining up with a security scanner. The scanners are set far enough away from the painting that they're not in your eyeline when viewing the artwork, but I assume they are both wirelessly connected to the alarm above the painting. Aiden and Frankie step right up to the scanners and a blue light scans their retinas simultaneously. Then I notice the green light above the painting turns red, presumably indicating the alarm has been rendered inactive.

Aiden hands Frankie a pair of pale blue gloves which I recognise as nitrile gloves. I keep a supply of these synthetic rubber gloves at home. They protect artwork against the sweat and oils in human skin and, in my case, they also protect my anonymity by ensuring I leave no fingerprints behind.

"Could you do the honours?" Aiden says to Frankie.

Frankie dons the gloves and then gingerly grips the frame either side and plucks the painting off the wall. Immediately my mind begins racing.

It's off the wall. It's unalarmed. Am I ever going to get a better opportunity than this, with only Aiden and a solitary security guard between me and the front door? I could shove Aiden to the ground, knee the guard in the balls, and then grab the painting and make a run for it.

Calm down, you idiot, I mentally chide myself. *That's far too risky. For a start, that guard isn't going to be taken out so easily and that painting looks too cumbersome for a quick getaway down all those stairs.*

"Set it down over there." Aiden nods towards the table.

Once the painting is on the table Aiden dismisses Frankie, who is clearly unnerved by having to leave the unalarmed painting, even though he'll be on guard downstairs. I hear his footsteps on the long L-shaped staircase and then there's silence. Leaning over the ornate balustrade, I observe him standing at the foot of the stairs, hands clasped in front of him, waiting to be called back up.

"He's still there," Aiden says behind me.

I turn around to face him. "Just making sure. I'd feel somehow responsible if it should go missing."

Aiden snorts. "I bet you would."

We gaze at each other for a few seconds. He's acting very odd today and making some weird comments. Maybe he's annoyed that his father has gone abroad with the sexy Hannah, leaving poor Aiden behind with the staff keeping a watchful eye over him.

Aiden reaches down beneath the table top to slide open the same slim drawer that he plucked the nitrile gloves from. He grabs another pair, as well as a small round object, handing the items to me. I glance down to see the round object is a jeweller's loupe—an eyepiece used to examine diamonds or, in this case, artwork.

"Knock yourself out," he says gesturing towards the painting.

I carefully don the gloves and then I grab the eyepiece and bend down, leaning over this most precious piece of art. I can't believe I'm this close to it. "Amazing!" I mumble as I study it through the magnifying effect of the loupe.

"Are you looking for anything specific?" Aiden asks.

"These wooden panels are sensitive to temperature and humidity changes, so over time you'd expect to see some signs of warping and cracking. The type of pigments used must also be contemporary with the period." My voice always sounds deeper to my own ears when I'm nervous, but I'm hoping Aiden doesn't pick up on that. I carefully lift the painting up at one side so I can get a glimpse of the back. "As I've already mentioned, the frame isn't original. It's too ornate and too wide, and it's independent of the crossbeam at the back, which means it wasn't part of the original design. I'd say the frame is late seventeenth century."

"Does that affect its value?" Aiden asks.

"Not at all," I tell him.

I lay the painting flat again and glance up at Aiden. "If anything it adds to the authenticity of the painting itself. You see, it was common practice during the Baroque period to replace old frames with ones that reflected the extravagant style of the grand houses of the time. Paintings like this, from the High Renaissance period, would have originally been housed in simple frames that were seen as plain and boring compared to the flamboyant style of the time."

"I see," Aiden replies. "Well, don't let me disturb you."

I return to my inspection as Aiden waits patiently behind me, allowing me several minutes of uninterrupted scrutiny while I mumble on about my findings. Eventually, though, there's only so much analysis even I can do with just a jeweller's loupe. I stand up and arch my back, stretching out my back muscles.

"Well?" Aiden asks.

I turn to face him. "It definitely has centuries of age to it, but to be more precise than that I'd need to take it away for radiocarbon analysis and possibly a forensic examination using an infrared scanner."

"What would infrared tell you?"

"Infrared can see through the layers and show any restoration work, which might prove it's genuine if you know the provenance of the piece and if the reparation has been properly documented. Although I doubt this particular piece came with any paperwork so that wouldn't be of much value here. However, infrared can also see through to the under-drawing and that could tell us an awful lot. That's where a pencil or charcoal sketch was made before the artist began. Often, in the case of a forgery, the under-drawing appears too formal. By that I mean instead of a freehand drawing you might see gridlines, which helps a forger exactly replicate the composition of the original."

"But with your own expert eye you haven't found anything that would lead you to believe it's anything but genuine."

"No. In fact, everything I've seen so far has been very encouraging."

"Well then, if that's satisfied your curiosity, I think we'd better put it back now, don't you?"

I groan inwardly. *Aiden, you're such a tease. Do we really have to?*

Of course, I knew I was never going to be allowed to take the painting away with me for further examination, but if I'm staying the night, hopefully I'll get a chance to study their security system in more detail. "Yes," I say with a reluctant sigh, "I suppose we'd better put it back. Frankie must be wetting himself down there."

Aiden laughs. "Why don't you shout him back up?"

I walk over to the staircase and lean over the balustrade, calling down to Frankie. "Hey Frankie, you'll never believe it. Aiden's just done a runner with the painting."

He looks up at me with panic in his eyes, not sure whether to believe me or not.

"I'm just kidding," I assure him. "You can put it back now."

"Very funny, sir," he grumbles as he makes his way up the long staircase.

It's while Frankie is hanging the painting back on the wall that I notice something curious that makes my heart judder in disbelief. I spot an obvious flaw in the alarm system. I'm utterly gobsmacked that such an error could go undetected. I can't believe my luck. I have to physically restrain myself from throwing a fist pump in the air. This changes everything. I can fast-track this now. Looks like I'll be doing more than just an inspection tonight.

22 – AIDEN

I breathe a sigh of relief, glad the painting is back on the wall. For a moment there I thought Mackenzie might run off with it, but everything went to plan. I can do this. I *really* think I can do this. Now to put Phase Two of my plan into operation.

I know what my dad would say—that I watch too many movies—and he'd be right. I *do* live in a fantasy world, but that tends to happen when your reality sucks. I can't stand the status quo anymore.

Well, I was looking for something to spice up my life and this is definitely going to do that. In fact it's going to completely change my life forever. There'll be no going back once it's done and that excites me, but I'm also utterly terrified at the same time. I have to stay strong and see this through.

I'm not my father's son anymore.

I'm a twenty-two-year-old man.

I know my own mind.

It's time to emancipate the real Aiden Foxwell.

23 – MACKENZIE

Once the painting is back on the wall, Aiden dismisses Frankie. "That will be all," he says, and Frankie nods.

I wait for Frankie to leave, my heart still racing, and then I turn to Aiden, hoping to nudge some additional information out of him if I can. "Impressive alarm system."

"My dad insisted on a dual-controlled alarm for each individual painting. It would take forever to steal the whole collection."

"But not too long to steal a single painting."

"Maybe not, but you'd still need two people to deactivate each alarm. And not just *any* people."

"No. People with the correct eyeballs."

"That's right, Mackenzie. So how are you going to do it?"

My heart lurches making me gasp out loud. *Shit! What did he just say? How am I going to do it?*

"Do what?"

"Steal the Raphael, of course."

Aiden stares me straight in the eyes and we stand like that, in silence, for several long seconds before Aiden speaks up again. "I know how *I'd* do it."

"How?" I ask cautiously, wondering where on earth this is leading.

"I'd befriend the gay son, wait for him to invite me to stay over, and then I'd sneak into his room for a night of unbridled passion."

"Really?" I snort. "Is that your wet dream in a nutshell? To have a thief sneak into your bedroom and take your virginity?"

"I'm not a virgin," he snaps.

"And after this hypothetical fornication takes place, what then?"

"The son is exhausted by the sexually-demanding thief and falls into a deep sleep."

I quirk an eyebrow. "Sexually demanding? Do you have this fantasy often?"

"Nightly," he sneers.

"So, the son falls asleep and then what?"

"It's obvious, isn't it?"

"No."

"The thief plucks his eyeball out."

My lip curls in disgust. "After they've just shagged? Heartless bastard this thief, isn't he?"

"It's the only way," Aiden replies gleefully, as if he's enjoying discussing supposed tactics with me. No doubt he thinks he's got me on the back foot by making me aware he suspects me.

"There's a flaw in your logic, Aiden. No matter how deep the sleep, I'm certain you'd notice if I plucked your eyeball out. It'd sting quite a bit. I can't have you making a commotion."

"I'll try not to make too much fuss," he replies without missing a beat, a smirk spreading across his face.

He's one cool customer, I'll give him that. He must think he's got the upper hand somehow. All I can do is play along for now and see where this leads.

"And then I suppose I'd have to sleep with Frankie because I'd need his eyeball too."

"Good luck with that. He's straight. But there's something else you've overlooked."

"What's that?"

"Your arms aren't long enough to scan both eyeballs at the same time. The scanners are set too wide apart."

"That's easy. All I'd have to do is mount each eyeball on a long stick, like a pair of toasting marshmallows."

Aiden grunts. "That's gross, Mackenzie. But all joking aside, how are you *really* going to do it?"

I give him a hard stare. This feels like an absurd game of truth or dare, but the only one who's risking anything is me. Maybe he's already called the police and he's keeping me talking until they arrive. But then why the charade of taking the painting off the wall for me to examine? And what am I going to be charged with, attempting to authenticate a work of art? I'm an art historian. It's hardly a crime. None of this makes any sense. *Why don't I just ask him what's going on?*

"If you think I'm here to steal the painting, why show it to me and why show me how the alarm works?"

"Maybe I'm bored. Maybe I'm dying to see you in action."

"It's not a spectator sport," I sneer.

"Pity. Okay, so tell me the plan. I won't say a word to anyone, I promise."

"Do you seriously expect me to believe that you'd allow someone to steal your inheritance simply because you're bored?"

"Well, I only get noticed when I'm a bad boy. If I behave no-one pays me any attention at all."

"But you haven't been a bad boy, have you, Aiden?"

"Oh but I have. I'm an accessory now, you see. I've aided and abetted. I've shown you the painting, as well as showing you how our security system works. What else do you want me to do, steal it for you?"

"That would be nice."

"I can do the next best thing. I'll be your inside man."

"I don't need an inside man."

"Yes you do, but it's only fair to warn you that I'd have to disavow all knowledge of this conversation if we got caught."

"Disavow?" I scoff. "Get a grip, Aiden. You've been watching too many movies."

"Movies are a great educator of the masses. Let me help."

"I work alone."

"Please!"

"No."

"What about the security camera?" Aiden nods up to the wall-mounted lens staring straight back at us. "You'll need someone to fix that for you."

"Is it on all the time?"

"I know what you're thinking. You think we might need to insert a blank loop into the live feed so it's showing some old piece of boring footage instead of the actual robbery. Am I right?"

I shake my head in disbelief. "It's frightening how into this you are."

"It's okay, the camera isn't on all the time. It only flicks on when someone passes within range of its motion sensor and the feedback isn't monitored. It's only there in case something goes missing so we can hand the footage over to the police. All it needs is for someone to delete the incriminating section of footage after you've made your escape and before anyone notices the painting is missing. That's a job for your inside man. Leave it with me."

I gaze at him, momentarily dumbstruck. He's obviously trying to manipulate me in some way but I'm not sure how or why or what Aiden thinks he's going to get out of this. He wouldn't be helping me steal from his father just to get attention. That doesn't add up. There's something else going on here and Aiden isn't letting on what it is.

"You can't be serious."

"Deadly serious," he assures me, even though there's a hint of amusement in his eyes.

"You're poking fun at me."

"No I'm not! You need to learn the difference between my serious face and my teasing face."

"Okay. How about you show me your teasing face and I'll punch it so I can tell your two faces apart?"

"That's not nice, Mackenzie."

"Then stop messing with me."

"I'm not. Are we on for tonight?"

"On? What do you mean? You want me to

sneak into your bedroom?"

He rolls his eyes. "No. I want you to steal the painting."

"Oh, I see," I sneer. "So that's why I received an invite to stay the night. And there I was thinking my luck was in."

Aiden moves in close and looks me right in the eyes. "Don't be discouraged by this turn of events," he says in a throaty purr. "I'm actually finding you more attractive by the minute, but you need to be patient. I'm keeping my powder dry until I've seen how you operate. I want you to impress me, Mackenzie."

My jaw stiffens. "I'm not a performing monkey," I growl. "Your Lordship can go fuck himself."

"Don't speak to me in that gruff tone," he purrs, leaning in closer still. "You're making me all goosebumpy."

24 – AIDEN

This is the third day in a row it's rained solidly. It seems fitting. My mood is about as damp and dreary as the view from the drawing room window. Mackenzie didn't stay over last night. We kissed on the gallery landing, but it was more of a punishment from him, leaving my lips swollen and bruised. Then he pushed me away and left. He'll be back, I'm certain of it. The painting is too important to him. I messaged him, inviting him over for dinner again tonight, but he hasn't responded yet. He's making me wait because he's annoyed with me. I'm the one who should be annoyed. He's using me. He has no right to be mad at me because I found him out.

Anyway, I don't suppose it matters exactly *when* he takes the painting, as long as it's before my dad gets back from Canada; although I'd rather just get on with it. I'll just be sat around twiddling my thumbs until the deed is done.

I saunter over to the corner of the drawing room, to where the upright piano is tucked against the wall, out of the way. I slide onto the worn leather seat. I don't bother lifting the piano lid. I could never play, but sitting here reminds me of my mum and the many hours she spent trying to teach me.

I wish I could have that time back. I'd practice day and night just to make her happy.

Hung on the wall above the piano is a

photograph of my parents on their wedding day. I don't know why it's been moved. It used to be hung over the fireplace—a more fitting display position for a photograph of the happiest day of a person's life. Maybe it brings back painful memories for my dad. Or maybe it's tucked out of the way in deference to his new lady friend. There used to be lots of smaller framed photographs of my mum scattered around the house, but not anymore. They've all been shoved in the side cabinet and replaced with photographs of Dad and Hannah.

Tears prick my eyes and I stand and rub them away with the back of my hand. There's too much history engrained within the walls of this house. I feel the weight of it all around me. This isn't a home, it's a time capsule of things gone by. It always felt that way to me, even when I was growing up. I treasured every moment we weren't here. I used to love the family's annual trip to Camber Sands on the south coast. It's where my mum grew up. Dad never took me there again after she died. Her parents were still living on the south coast at the time of her death but they moved to Australia shortly after. My grandparents on my dad's side both died when I was young, so I don't remember much about them. For the past seven years it's just been me and my dad and he's spent the entire time consoling himself with one lady friend after another. I'm glad to say he seems to have settled on one now, but all through my teens I felt I'd been set adrift in a rudderless boat.

I alternate between acting up and feeling sorry for myself, but I'm old enough now to break out of this rut I've been stuck in. I have to make a life of my own, away from here.

I move over to the side cabinet and flop down on the rug in front of it, dragging one of the heavy leather-bound photograph albums out onto the floor. I sit cross-legged, slowly turning its pages, falling into an even darker melancholy as the memories come flooding back, but one image manages to make me smile. It's from the very last trip we took as a family to Camber Sands when I was fifteen. I'm not sure who took the picture. It could have been Grandma Ellis or it might just as easily have been a complete stranger. My mum was like that—a very friendly and outgoing person. She probably asked a passer-by to take the snap. You can tell it was taken in the moment. We're not standing in a formal pose. My little dog at the time—a pug called Yoda—is jumping up my leg and my mum is standing behind me, her arms around me, tickling my ribs to make me giggle. I never used to smile for the camera, so this was her way of making me say "cheese." It's a delightful portrait of mother and son, only slightly marred by the fact my dad is standing behind us, scowling at us. He was probably worried the stranger might run off with his expensive camera. That photograph is actually the perfect metaphor for my relationship with my dad. He's always been in the background of my life, looking on disapprovingly.

Maybe that's unfair. Mum and I were so tight, he couldn't really help but feel left out, but then he never put the effort in to try to redress the balance.

I pluck the photograph off the page and shove it in my pocket before placing the album back in its slot in the cabinet. And then I go to my bedroom and pack. I get everything I need in a single suitcase. I pull the photograph from my pocket and place it carefully on top of my packed clothes before closing the lid. Then I shove the suitcase at the back of my wardrobe, out of sight, until I need it.

It's all down to Mackenzie now.

25 - MACKENZIE

The flaw in the security system had become apparent to me when Frankie hung the painting back up on the wall. It's a stupid schoolboy error by whoever installed the system—almost unbelievable, in fact—and the more I think about it, the more my suspicions are aroused. After the bizarre conversation with Aiden yesterday, it feels too much like a trap.

The sensors that trip the alarm should be evenly spaced behind the wooden panel that the portrait was painted onto, but they're only pointing at the left and right edges of the frame. That makes my life easy. All I have to do is detach the artwork from its frame, leaving the frame on the wall and the sensors undisturbed.

I'm convinced I'm being played but I can't for the life of me make sense of it. Not unless it's one of those stupid risk assessment plans, where they try to encourage someone to steal something just to find out how good their security is. Or maybe Aiden wants me to steal his father's painting as an act of revenge for trying to marry him off. But that would be *some* act of revenge. I'm not really sure what's going on in Aiden's head, but if he's actively encouraging me to steal the painting, I can't see him hanging around afterwards to take the flak. He must be planning on leaving home. Maybe he's leaving home whether or not I go through with this, which means my window of opportunity could be limited. Once Aiden's gone, I won't have access to the house anymore.

Aiden's invited me over for dinner this evening and once again he said I can stay the night. He made it abundantly clear we'll be in separate rooms. Maybe it was all that talk of me gouging his eyeball out that's put a dampener on his ardour.

I've just messaged him back to say I'll be there.

So, I guess tonight is the big night and so this will be our farewell dinner.

Tonight I steal the Raphael and then I shall never again set foot in Foxwell Manor. I'll miss Aiden. He's been a worthy distraction, but I'm not a man to carry excess baggage with me. The reality of our situation is that Aiden's looking for a more enduring relationship than I'm willing to offer. That doesn't stop me getting hot under the collar for him, but it's all in vain. I very much doubt I'll be able to tempt him into a quick shag, not even as a parting gift.

26 – AIDEN

Dinner was awful. Not the food, but the oppressive atmosphere. Mackenzie sat staring at me all night. I wasn't sure whether he wanted to tell me something or ask me something, but it seems neither of us dare put into words all the thoughts that are running through our minds.

He hasn't said as much, but I can feel in my bones that tonight is the night.

I don't usually drink brandy, but after dinner I join Mackenzie in a nightcap, and then it's time to show him to his room. It's nowhere near mine. I've allocated him the closest bedroom to the gallery landing.

We stand toe-to-toe outside his bedroom door, his gaze drilling into me. I know what his eyes are asking me, but I daren't. If I go into that room with him, I'll come out of there compromised in a way I don't know if I could cope with, all things considered. My judgement is already impaired as far as Mackenzie is concerned. I'm trying my best to keep a level head and I know sleeping with him is the last thing I should do.

"I have something for you," I say, grabbing his hand and flipping it over so I can place the small gift box in his palm.

He glances down at it. "What's this?"

"It's for luck."

He opens the box and scowls. "It's a seashell."

"Yes. A tellin shell from Camber Sands. I've

had it since I was a boy. It's very special to me, but I want *you* to have it."

"Me? What on earth for?"

My heart pangs. "Don't you want it?"

"No. Yes. I mean, it's very...touching...thank you."

"Take good care of it, won't you?"

Mackenzie nods and closes the lid, slipping the box into his trouser pocket. "I suppose I should have got you something too."

"No, it's okay."

He gazes into my eyes. "Well, I guess this is it, Aiden?"

"I guess so."

He leans in closer. "So, do I get a kiss?"

Without waiting for my response, Mackenzie pulls me to him and moulds his lips to mine. I wrap my arms around him, our bodies crushing together so I can feel the gift box pressing against my hip, as well as his arousal. Our brandy-soaked tongues writhe together, making me quiver inside, and his hands slide down my back to grope my arse cheeks. His lips pull free of mine but only so he can press his mouth to my ear and talk dirty.

"You didn't eat much of your dinner. Were you saving yourself so you could gorge on my juicy todger?"

I snort out a laugh. "Juicy! Are you leaking, Mr. Oden?"

"There might be a drop of two of pre-spillage for your delectation. Shall I get a spoon or are you going to drink straight from the font?"

"Stop!" I say on a fit of giggles. "You're making

me salivate."

"Well, I wouldn't want you to go hungry." He reaches for his fly, but I still his hand.

"We can't."

"Of course we can," he mutters huskily between pressing a row of urgent kisses down the side of my neck. "We're both adults."

"Yes but we really shouldn't, Mackenzie," I insist, pushing him away. "We both need to keep a level head."

"Come on, Aiden," he begs. "Just a quickie."

"No!"

He groans and heaves a long sigh. "I suppose you're right."

"Listen, you don't have to worry about the security footage. I'll take care of that."

"I damn well hope so. I'm relying on you."

"Do you have a getaway car or do you need me to drive you somewhere?"

"What? No!" He rubs his brow, looking flustered, as if he's still trying to regain his composure after the kiss. "Stop fretting, Aiden. I *have* done this before, you know. It's very kind of you to offer but I've hired a car."

"Sorry. I'm just a bit on edge. I've never aided and abetted anyone before. My nerves are jangling."

"You know you don't have to get involved with this. I can deal with the security camera footage myself if you just tell me where it's stored."

"No. I said I'll handle it and I will."

"If you're sure."

"I'm positive. Oh and that reminds me, I've left

a linen tablecloth draped over the banister. You might find it useful to wrap something up in."

Mackenzie smiles. "Very thoughtful."

"So, it's all systems go then."

He nods. "I wonder how things would have turned out if we'd met under different circumstances."

"I've been wondering about that too. We've always had this thing in the way, haven't we? This stupid painting of a man who's been dead for 500 years. It's tainted every moment we've been together."

Mackenzie shrugs. "But if we're honest, we were always after different things. I'm not the sort of man you fall in love with."

"You're wrong. You're *exactly* the sort of man I could fall for."

"No, Aiden. You want the fantasy version of me. The one who sweeps you off your feet and treats you like a prince. You want hearts and flowers. You don't want me."

"I don't think you're so heartless as you imagine yourself to be." I jab my finger into his chest. "I think there's a soft spot in there with my name on it."

He huffs. "You'll see how heartless I am when I walk out of the front door with your inheritance tucked under my arm. You're a special person, Aiden. Too good for me. I hope you find what you're looking for." He turns and moves towards the bedroom door, pausing at the entrance. "Goodbye, Aiden Foxwell."

"I don't do goodbyes," I tell him. "The future hasn't been written yet. Sometimes the end is just the beginning."

He gazes at me in an oddly avuncular way before offering up some reassuring pearls of wisdom. "Don't fret it, Aiden. A goodbye is simply the start of a new chapter. You're still young. There are plenty of chapters to be written yet. You have so much to look forward to. You'll find the right man for you one day."

27 – MACKENZIE

My alarm wakes me in the dead of the night, setting my heart racing. I take a few moments to gather my senses and then roll out of bed and quickly dress. I try my best to simply go through the motions as if it's any other job. I fill my pockets with my phone, wallet, flick-knife and the gift box Aiden gave me with the good luck charm in it. I pull on my woollen beanie—the one with the flashlight built in— and don a pair of nitrile gloves.

I'm all set, but...this feels weird. I'm getting a knot in my stomach. I've never been conflicted about stealing anything before, but tonight I am. This is Aiden's inheritance and he doesn't seem to give a damn. I wonder about the boy's sanity, but then I sometimes wonder about my own. I suppose we're all a bit crazy in our own way.

The members of staff are so very discreet in this place you rarely see anyone unless you summon them, so I'm not expecting to bump into anyone on my night-time stroll. Aiden's father is in Canada with his lady friend, although to be fair the only time I've seen him here at the manor was on that first night when he more or less warned me off Aiden. No wonder the boy's losing his mind. He's left rattling around this big old house with just the staff for company, while his father is off gallivanting with Hannah Reece.

I'm truly going to miss Aiden. He's a fine young man. He deserves better than this. I hope he finds the balls to leave this place and make a life

147

for himself.

I grab the wooden chair from my bedroom and make my way along the landing to the gallery. Moments later I'm standing in front of the Raphael. I reach in my pocket for my flick-knife. Despite the high-tech security set-up, this is all the equipment I'm going to need tonight.

I climb up onto the chair, aware the security camera is tracking my every move. I pray Aiden knows what he's doing and actually remembers to delete the footage before anyone realises the painting is missing. My flashlight illuminates the painting, its blue-white light draining the colour out of the artist's strokes, making the tones appear cold when they were warm in the natural daylight. I hold the frame steady as I slide my knife between it and the wooden panel behind. I twist my wrist and cringe as the wood creaks. Pausing to take a few calming breaths, I slowly withdraw the knife. Inch by inch, I move around the frame, sliding the knife in, twisting and releasing, and all the while I feel a pair of watchful eyes on me. I spare a glance for the young man in the painting. The young Raphael. He's observing my every move. *"Careful, now,"* I can hear him saying.

It's embarrassing to have the great master watching me at work. This is the most low-tech heist I've ever attempted and the irony is the security system is the most high-tech I've encountered. It feels like someone—Aiden— deliberately circumvented the security system to allow me access.

"Very sorry about this," I say to Raphael, "but this isn't even your frame. I mean look at it. It's hideous. I promise I'll find something more fitting

148

to frame you in."

Eventually the painting is free of its frame and I slide it carefully down the wall. It's big and clumsy, but not so bad as when it was in its frame. I deposit it on the table and grab the linen cloth Aiden left out for me. I wrap the painting in the cloth before removing my gloves. With the painting tucked under my armpit and held securely at the bottom, I gingerly make my way down the stairs, careful not to trip. I don't bother collecting my overnight bag. There's nothing in there I can't easily replace and I'm sure Aiden will get rid of it for me in the morning.

Leaving Foxwell Manor for the last time, I open the back door of the hire car and slide the painting into the rear footwell. Then I set off at speed, up the long driveway, wondering if Aiden's watching me make my escape.

And what of him? What of Aiden?

Surely he can't stay at Foxwell Manor after tonight. But where will he go?

28 – AIDEN

From my bedroom window I watch Mackenzie's car lights disappear into the distance, and then I set the next phase of my plan into action. I tidy up the area around the painting, putting the chair back in Mackenzie's room and grabbing his overnight bag which he's left behind. I shove his bag at the back of my wardrobe and grab my own ready-packed suitcase.

Making my way downstairs, I head straight for Frankie's office, where all the surveillance monitoring equipment is fed back to. I quickly locate the relevant recording and transfer it off the hard drive onto a flash drive, checking there are no other copies stored anywhere else. I pocket the flash drive and then write Frankie a quick note telling him I'm going on a road trip for a couple of weeks.

It's time to make my own escape. Jessica—my super racy car—has been waiting patiently out front, where I parked her earlier. I toss my suitcase onto the back seat and then I set off into the night.

I love driving in the small hours. It's the only time Jessica can really let her hair down. She gobbles up the miles and three hours later I'm in my favourite place in the whole world—Camber Sands on the south coast. I check into The Dunlin, splashing out on a platinum room, which means a top floor room with a sea view and a balcony. I have a feeling my next credit card bill is going to be a tad inflated when it comes in. I'm in celebration mode.

I throw open the French doors that lead to the balcony and breathe in the salty sea air. After the recent rain, the wind changed direction, and now it's drawing warm air up from the tropics for a last taste of summer before autumn truly sets in. Already I can see dawn beginning to break in the eastern sky. I leave the doors open and hop into bed, hoping to grab a couple of hours sleep.

29 – MACKENZIE

I slept with the painting in bed with me last night. My flat in Islington doesn't feel worthy of this masterpiece and I'll be glad to get it off my hands. Imagine if someone were to break in and steal it without even realising its true worth. Now that would be a really fucked-up piece of irony after all I've been through. Not to mention the fact I'm already down ten grand, plus the grand it cost to hire the Bentley, as well as the hotel and taxi fares.

Fortunately, I don't have long to wait to shift it. Lenny is coming round in an hour to take the painting off my hands. As I recall, the buyer for this one is Lenny's Russian oligarch friend who goes by the codename Morozko. Morozko's representative here in London will meet up with Lenny to arrange the transaction. He'll have his own art expert with him to verify the authenticity of the work and then Lenny will confirm the bank transfer before officially handing the painting over.

Once that happens, I'm out of here. Officially retired, I'll be in search of the perfect slice of paradise where I can live out the rest of my natural days in blissful ignorance of the world around me.

So why am I feeling so morose?

I know why.

It's because I can't get Aiden off my mind.

I take the seashell he gave me out of its box

and set it down on the coffee table. This is the first time I've studied it in the daylight and now I can see its delicate pink and yellow stripes. I don't normally collect trinkets, but I can't bring myself to dispose of this one. I wish I could return it to him. It's a nice keepsake of the brief time we spent together, but I'm not worthy of such a gift when Aiden made it clear it held deep sentimental value for him.

This shift in my emotional state is really quite disturbing. Why am I behaving so toe-curlingly mushy over Aiden? I don't recognise the man I'm turning into. If this is what happens to a man when he starts caring, I've done well to avoid it all these years. He's not even my type. I don't usually go for the young and the beautiful because they tend to be vacuous. But Aiden's different. He's witty and intelligent and I've enjoyed mentally sparring with him.

Something he said last night keeps nudging at my brain. I try to focus in on it. Oh yes, that's it. I remember now.

"Sometimes the end is just the beginning."

It's an odd thing to say, that's why it stuck in my mind. What could he have possibly meant by it? I can picture his face as he said it, his gaze so strong and true, and I can't help wondering where he is now. I feel for him, out there somewhere, alone and maybe a little bit scared. I wonder if he's thinking of me too.

30 – AIDEN

It's been two days since the theft of the painting and all's well. I've had no emergency phone calls from anyone at the manor, so no-one suspects anything yet, and I'm assuming Frankie must have got my note about me going on a road trip for a couple of weeks, so no-one's wondering where I am either.

As for Mackenzie, I wasn't really expecting to hear from him yet. Not in the immediate aftermath, anyway. I suspect his main priority will be to keep a low profile until he's offloaded the painting. He won't want to hang onto it for too long though, so I imagine I'll be hearing from him pretty soon. I'm sure he'll be dying to speak with me.

In the meantime, I'm taking a leisurely breakfast on the balcony in my hotel room in Camber Sands, watching the dog walkers criss-crossing the sand dunes. My phone is sitting next to my glass of orange juice, within easy reach, should he call. I can't help staring at it, willing it to make some sort of noise. Patience has never been my strong suit.

Finally it pings just as a gull flies overhead, cawing so noisily that I might have missed the message alert if I hadn't been so focused on my phone.

I hesitate.

My gut is doing a jig. I'm so excited to hear from him and yet so nervous of his reaction that

I'm almost afraid to pick it up.

Play it cool, Aiden, I tell myself. *That's all you have to do. Play it cool.*

I grab my phone and tap the screen to open up the waiting message.

Mackenzie: *Where are you?*

I stare at the message. *Short and to the point!* Taking a deep breath, I key in a zingy response.

Aiden: *Hi honey. I've reserved a table for lunch. The oysters are to die for.*

I chew nervously on my bottom lip as I await his response. *Brace for impact*, I tell myself. I don't have long to wait.

Mackenzie: *Don't you honey me, you little shit.*

Aiden: *That's no way to speak to your partner in crime.*

Mackenzie: *Where are you hiding?*

Aiden: *Not hiding. Chilling. In a lovely little hotel on the south coast. You'll adore it.*

Mackenzie: *I'll need more than that.*

Aiden: *Here's the link.* [The Dunlin Hotel]. *I'm in Room 30. I'll expect roses.*

31 - MACKENZIE

I purchase a bunch of roses and then set off in my hire car for the two-hour drive to Camber Sands on the south coast, where Aiden is holed up. I locate the hotel easily enough and pull into the car park at the rear. Grabbing the bunch of flowers from the passenger seat, I stride into reception, holding the stems irreverently by the base, the pink buds almost brushing the floor. The brunette behind the desk looks up as I approach, her gaze sweeping over me like a medical scanner, recording every muscle and bulge. She flicks her long hair over her shoulder and slides her tongue over her cerise lips, but her flirty behaviour is wasted on me this morning.

I mutter a terse "Hello!" and in return she greets me with a bullish smile and an incorrect assumption.

"Good morning, sir, and welcome! Have you stayed at The Dunlin before?"

"Sorry, no, I'm not checking in. I'm visiting a..." My lip curls involuntarily as I try to find the right word to describe him. *A weasel, a louse, a snake in the grass. A fucked-up little—*

"Sorry, sir?" the brunette says, interrupting my train of thought. "You're visiting a what?"

I steel myself. "Friend," I grind out stiff-jawed.

"Oh, of course. Name?"

"Foxwell. Room 30"

"And *your* name, sir?

157

"Mr. Oden."

"Just a moment." She calls his room. "There's a Mr. Oden in reception to see you." She nods as she listens to his response through the tiny headset she's wearing, her eyes flicking over the bunch of roses dangling from my hand. When she's finished the call she points me in the direction of the lift. "Top floor, turn left and it's at the end of the corridor."

I mumble a thank you and then proceed with haste to the lift, but it's so sedate I'm certain the stairs would have been the quicker option. I imagine it's designed with retirees in mind, so as not to give them a heart attack as they scale the dizzying heights of this low-rise seaside hotel. Finally it deposits me on the third floor and I march to the end of the corridor, to the door marked *30*.

Before I have a chance to hammer my fist against it, the door swings open and I storm into the room with Aiden backing up in front of me.

"It's a fake," I bark, tossing the bunch of roses at him. He catches them as they hit him in the chest.

"It's nice to see you too," he says with a nervous smile. He glances down at the roses and his face drops. "They're plastic."

"I thought it appropriate," I snarl. "Fake painting, fake boyfriend, fake flowers." My jaw aches from pent-up rage. I must have been gnashing my teeth all the way from London.

He flings the roses on the bed. "You're mean, Mackenzie. That's no way to treat your inside man."

"What the hell is your game? Why did you want

158

me to steal a fake?"

"That 'fake' is a seventeenth-century copy. It's a precious work of art in its own right."

"It's by an unknown artist. It's worth peanuts compared to the Raphael." I press my hands to my hips, feeling like I need something to grip onto other than Aiden's throat. "Why did you go out of your way to convince me it was the genuine article?"

"I had my reasons."

"They'd better be damn good reasons."

He tilts his chin up defiantly. His eyes are ablaze, his lips plump and red, and his breath shallow. He's either sexually aroused or scared I'm going to hit him. Maybe I should throw him on the bed and find out which.

"You don't seriously think I was going to trust you with the real one, do you? I like you, Mackenzie, I like you a lot, but a thief is hardly the trustworthy type."

"Whoa, hold on a minute! Real one?"

"Yes."

"So you know where the real one is?"

He nods. "I know exactly where it is."

"Well?" I demand impatiently.

"Don't worry about it, Mackenzie. I have everything under control." He nods towards the open French doors. "We should be celebrating. Come and have a drink with me."

"Celebrating what? Where is the real one, Aiden?"

"*I* have it, of course."

"You?"

"Yes."

"Of course," I repeat wearily, rubbing my brow where a nerve is pulsing like it's about to explode out of my head and splatter blood all over the hotel carpet. "The boy wonder has it. I should have known."

Aiden gives me a sympathetic pout. "You look like hell. Come on, let me get you that drink."

I follow him out onto the balcony where there are a couple of rattan chairs and a glass-topped table. On the table sits two champagne flutes and a bottle of bubbly on ice.

"It's eleven in the morning," I point out, taking a seat.

"So what? I've been looking forward to seeing you again. I'm in the mood to celebrate. I had to start without you. You're already a glass behind."

He lifts the bottle from the ice bucket and fills both of the champagne flutes, sliding one over towards me. "Cheers!" he says raising his glass and taking a sip.

"Do you want to run this by me from the top?"

Aiden sets his glass back down. "We make a good team, don't we? I'm the brains and you're the brawn."

I grunt. "You're asking for a thick lip. Don't push your luck, I'm not in the best of moods. I need answers."

"Okay, Mackenzie, what do you want to know?"

"I told you. Start from the top."

"Really? You haven't figured *any* of this out?" He shakes his head, demonstrating his disappointment in me. "You're going *right* downhill in my estimation."

160

I jump to my feet and drag him out of his chair, pinning him against the side wall of the balcony with the force of my bodyweight. I shove my fist in his face, barely able to restrain myself from knocking his teeth out.

"I have had just about enough of you and that smart mouth of yours, you little shit. You'd better stop jerking me off, or you're going to need a new passport photo when I've finished rearranging your features."

Aiden stares at me wide-eyed. "Oh wow, Mackenzie! That was amazing. You've got that down pat. If I didn't know better, I'd swear you were a proper criminal."

"I *am* a proper criminal."

"I mean like a mafia boss or something. It was brilliant. Go on, do it again. Especially the part about rearranging my features."

I roll my eyes and release him. "For fuck's sake," I grumble as I slump back into my chair. "Has anyone ever told you how infuriating you are? There's no wonder your father abdicated his parental responsibilities to Frankie. You're too much of a bloody handful." I grab the glass of champagne and down it in one go.

"I'm not a kid. I don't need my dad anymore. I need someone who understands the way my mind works."

"You should check yourself into the psycho ward for the criminally insane. You'll find plenty of like-minded individuals there."

"You're just annoyed that I figured out what you were up to and changed the rules."

I grunt. "Am I supposed to be impressed?"

"Come on, Mackenzie," he whines. "Don't be

161

mad at me. I didn't do any of this out of malice. I did it because I need you and I was afraid that once you had the painting I'd never see you again."

"Need me? What for?"

"Because I'm a coward, Mackenzie. This is my one chance of getting free of my dad and the future he's got mapped out for me, but I daren't do it without you by my side. I don't know how to survive alone. I need someone who understands the way the world works. I need *you*, Mackenzie, because I've …"

"You've what?"

"Damn!" he mutters to himself, looking away. "This was so much easier when I practised it in the mirror this morning."

I snort. "You practised your little speech in front of the mirror?"

"Don't laugh at me."

"Come on. Just spit it out."

"I've been attracted to you since the day we met." Aiden's cheeks blaze with colour and I can't help but snicker at his awkwardness.

"I told you not to laugh," he whines.

"Sorry, but clearly that hurt, having to admit that out loud."

"It did. Very much so. Can I take it back?"

"I'm afraid not. It's out there now."

"Shit!" he sips some more champagne.

"I don't understand. If you have the real painting, why did you need me to steal the fake?"

"I didn't have the real one to begin with. I only had the fake. And now you've got the fake and I have the real one."

I rub my brow at the spot where a migraine is forming. "I'm not following any of this."

"Look, Mackenzie. I have to know if we can make this work or not."

"Make what work?"

"I'd like us to be partners."

I raise an eyebrow. "You mean like bed partners?"

Aiden hesitates before answering. "Well, the exact terms of this partnership have yet to be negotiated."

I nod towards the room. "So how about we jump into that fancy hotel bed of yours and get down to the nitty-gritty of these negotiations, so I can find out exactly what it is you want from me?"

"We don't have to have sex to know how we feel about each other."

I scowl at him like he's talking crap. "I think we do."

He sighs. "You're so predictable, Mackenzie. You've been gagging to get me between the sheets ever since you won that auction."

"No. I've been gagging to slip between your cheeks but I don't care *where* we do it. We can do it on the floor if you like."

"Don't be crass. I'm not a roll-in-the-hay type of boy. You're not going to get anywhere with me if you disrespect me."

"Oh, His Lordship wants me to respect him," I scoff. "Well, maybe when you've finished double-crossing me I'll think about it. I'm still waiting for an explanation."

Aiden sighs. "Okay, listen carefully because I'm only saying this once. When we went up to the gallery landing to examine the painting, do you recall another painting on the floor, leaning against the wall near the table. It was covered in a cloth, like it was waiting to be hung."

I scrunch my nose up as I try to think back. "Vaguely, now that you mention it."

"That was the copy. I'd placed it there earlier in the day. I switched them over while you were bent over the balcony teasing Frankie about me running off with the painting. You were so close to the truth I had to bite my lip so I didn't laugh out loud."

"And did you also mess with the sensors on the alarm?"

"Yes. I did that while you were examining the original. I repositioned the sensors, so they were only pointing at the edge of the frame. I was hoping you'd spot that when the picture was being rehung and fortunately you did."

"It's my job to notice shit like that. But I still don't get why you needed me."

"The security system requires two authorised people to disable it, so I couldn't just take the painting without involving either Frankie or my dad."

"And in order to ask for their help you'd need a legitimate excuse for wanting to take the painting down," I offer.

"That's right," Aiden concurs.

"Like an art historian who wanted to examine the painting up close."

He nods. "Exactly."

"I see."

"I knew my dad would never agree to me having the painting down to show you, so it had to be Frankie. When my dad left for Canada it played right into my hands."

"So why haven't you been arrested yet? You're pretty conspicuous driving around in that DB11."

"Why would anyone arrest *me*? *You* stole the painting, not me."

"No I didn't, you switched..." It's in that moment that realisation dawns on me like a slap across the face. "Fuck me! I'm the fall guy."

"Brilliant, isn't it?" Aiden boasts.

"I hate you."

"It'll pass."

"Where did the fake come from?"

"Out of our storage closet at home."

"Why was there a fake in your storage closet?"

"I found out from my dad that the fake had always been hung on the wall when he was a kid. I didn't realise until all this happened that even my grandparents weren't averse to buying paintings on the black market. That copy may be by an unknown artist, but for decades it was the nearest thing the world had to the genuine article, so it was a museum piece in its own right, until it too was stolen. After it changed hands a few times, my family eventually purchased it. When my dad inherited the manor, he decided it wasn't fitting for a Foxwell to have a fake on the wall, so it was shoved in the closet, out of the way. But when he heard the original had resurfaced, he simply had to have it, no matter how much it cost. So you see, Mackenzie, a large portion of my family's fortune must now be tied up in that painting and I begrudge that."

"Why?"

"I'm the heir to that fortune and how am I ever going to release the value of that asset without getting involved with dodgy characters and being on the wrong side of the law? I figured I may as well get this problem resolved sooner rather than later, since you know people who can cash the painting in for me, and at least I'd have the money now, when I need it, rather than having to wait to inherit it. Basically, my dad put me in this awkward position, just so he could have bragging rights on a gallery landing that he maybe visits once a year when he has friends over at Christmas."

"Are you telling me there's an empty frame sitting on the wall at Foxwell Manor and no-one's noticed yet?"

"It's not empty. I took a photograph of the original, uploaded it to Quickie Prints and ordered a print to fit the size of the frame. From a distance it's hard to tell the difference. It could sit there for months before anyone notices."

"But if you already had the original, why did you need me to steal the fake? You could have just blamed the theft on me without having me go through that whole charade."

"Because I didn't just want the painting. I wanted the man too."

"I don't follow."

"Let's just say I needed the evidence of you stealing the painting as my insurance policy."

"Insurance against what?"

"In case you become...uncooperative."

"Uncooperative! Wait a second. What evidence?"

"The footage from the security camera."

My jaw almost drops to the floor. "You told me that you'd deal with the camera footage and I trusted you."

"I did deal with it, just not in the way you envisaged."

"You smart-arsed little runt."

"But you do see where this leaves us, don't you?"

"Yeah. In a hotel room, drinking champagne, when all I really want to do is skin you alive."

"You know it's not really me you're angry with. You're annoyed with yourself for getting taken in by my brilliant plotting. But don't worry, these negative feelings you're experiencing will soon pass. What you need to do now is focus on your future. You have a decision to make. Either you agree to my terms or I'm afraid I'll have to hand you in."

"Do what?"

"I think you'll find my terms are very fair and I hope that over these past few days I've proved myself worthy of you. I'm not some dumb kid. You can see that now, can't you? I need you to see me as an equal, Mackenzie. It's important to me."

"I'm sorry, I stopped listening after 'hand you in.'"

He rolls his eyes. "Look, I have no intention of calling the police unless you force me to. Right at this moment in time we have everything we need to make this work. Don't throw it all away because your ego got bruised. We can both come out of this as winners. I want us to be together, Mackenzie. I've never lived on my own. I've never had to stand on my own two feet. I need you."

"What you mean is you need someone with the right connections to cash in the painting."

"Well, that too," he admits coyly. "But the money doesn't mean anything to me if you don't come as part of the package."

"So basically you're blackmailing me into being your partner, whatever that entails. I'll tell you what it most definitely does *not* entail. It does *not* mean I'm your butler, your manservant, or the guy who holds the car door open for you while you prance around in those ridiculous Terminator sunglasses."

"Are you still ranting on about my sunglasses? I'll tell you what, if they bother you so much, why don't you buy me a new pair out of your half."

"My half?"

He nods. "I always intended to split the proceeds with you, if you agree to my terms."

"Really?" I gasp, my interest suddenly piqued. "You mean fifty-fifty?"

He nods. "That's what half usually means."

"Well, why didn't you say so in the first place?"

He smiles. "I like to have a few bargaining chips up my sleeve. A boy like me is used to always getting what he wants. So what do you say, Mackenzie? You see, I didn't really fool you. You're going to get your just desserts. You're entitled to half. We shared the risk and we can share the spoils. All you have to do is agree to be my partner."

168

My mind races, going over the options, but they appear to be thin on the ground and the truth is, I kind of like the sound of what he's offering. I'd already planned to retire and buy myself a private island somewhere, but wouldn't it be so much better if I had someone to share it with? A sexy young lover, perhaps? I don't know why I'm hesitating. I should snatch his hand off.

But first I need to set the ground rules. I'm not going to be bossed around by a twenty-two-year-old. I'm half his age again and that gives me seniority in this relationship. There's only room for one hand on the rudder and it's going to be mine.

"If we're going to do this, we do it *my* way."

"Okay," he says enthusiastically.

"Do you have your passport with you?"

"Yes. I packed everything. I don't plan on going back home. Why?"

"That's handy. And I always carry mine with me out of force of habit. A thief never knows when he's going to need to leave the country in a hurry."

Aiden scowls at me. "Leave the country?"

"Yes. Pack your bags. We're leaving on the first flight out of here."

"What? Why? No."

"I don't think it's wise to hang around waiting for someone to discover the Raphael's gone missing, do you? Besides, I have retirement plans, somewhere exotic."

"But...but we can't leave Jessica."

"Jessica?"

"My car."

"You're kidding, right?"

"No I'm not. I told you, it'll be Christmas before someone discovers the painting is missing. I'm not leaving Jessica. If you want to go abroad, we take the car with us."

I groan. "Okay, fine. If you want to start with a road trip and get that car out of your system, I'll accommodate your wishes for now, but where I plan on ending up, there won't be any roads. I'm intending to spend the rest of my days in a *no news, no shoes* type of destination."

Aiden gives a sarcastic huff. "Oh are you? Well, I'm glad you can accommodate my wishes *for now*, seeing as I'm the one with the real painting."

"Come on, let's get going. Ferry or tunnel?"

"Tunnel," Aiden replies.

"Grab your stuff then. The sooner we leave the country, the better I'll feel."

Aiden quickly packs and we're soon down in the hotel car park where Jessica stands out like a sore thumb, her roof down, as if she's catching the rays. He unlocks her and as I grab the fake painting out of my car, he holds the boot open and tells me to place it carefully on top of the other one that's already in there, wrapped in cloth. While he's tossing his suitcase on the back seat, I jump in the driver's seat.

"I've always wanted to drive one of these," I announce, a knot of excitement tugging at my gut.

I hear Aiden gasp but he doesn't say anything. Instead he walks around to the passenger side and slumps into the seat, slamming the door shut. As I pull out onto the main road he sits glaring at me, as if I've stolen his woman.

"What about *your* car?" he grunts. "Are you just going to leave it there?"

"I'll post the keys back to the hire company and get them to pick it up."

His eyes are still boring into me fifty minutes later, when we arrive at the Eurotunnel terminal in Folkestone. I pull up tight to the kerb at the check-in booth and Aiden groans and cover his eyes.

"What?" I ask.

"You'd better not scuff my Bridgestone alloys."

I chuckle to myself. He absolutely hates me being behind the wheel of his precious car and it gives me a nice warm feeling inside to make him sit there and suffer, after the way he's played me for a fool.

32 – AIDEN

By early afternoon we're driving off the shuttle train at Coquelles—a small town in northern France, just west of Calais. The crossing was fast but boring. Passengers stay in their car the whole time and there was nothing to see, as you'd expect in a tunnel. It was once we emerged on the other side that I began to have misgivings. Did I really want to leave England? This wasn't the way I envisaged things panning out. I wanted to buy a house in Camber Sands with Mackenzie, but maybe that was just another naive fantasy of mine. I'd planned everything up until the point Mackenzie and I met up at the hotel. Beyond that I had no real idea of what would happen. I couldn't predict Mackenzie's reaction so I had to play it by ear. I suppose it's only right that I let Mackenzie take charge—temporarily, at least. I've never stolen anything before. This whole idea of being *on the run* is new to me.

Well, I wanted some excitement and adventure in my life and Mackenzie has supplied that in spades. We've even agreed on a route—sort of. The rough plan so far, conceived in the tunnel, forty metres beneath the English Channel, is to make our way across Europe to Istanbul. The most direct route would be via Brussels, Cologne and Frankfurt, but we're in no particular rush, so we've decided to take the more scenic route through the Ardennes region.

Once we're on the open road, my mood

173

lightens. Jessica is made for this kind of journey. With the roof down and the sun on our faces, it feels like heaven, travelling through the idyllic countryside of the Ardennes with Mackenzie by my side. We wind our way through a deep wooded gorge, following the course of a glistening river, both wearing identical aviator shades that we picked up at the train terminal. In addition, Mackenzie is wearing a goofy grin, like he's having the time of his life at the wheel of *my* car. To be fair, it does wrap around him rather nicely and I kind of like to see *my man* at the wheel of a supercar, driving her like he was born to it. He accelerates into a bend, forcing the nose down and the tyres to grip, and Jessica glides around the arc like a dream.

I catch a whiff of Mackenzie's scent. "I like that cologne you're wearing."

"It's sandalwood," he shouts back at me above the noise of the engine and the air rushing by. "You like?"

"You smell good enough to eat and that's not fair because my stomach is rumbling. Are we stopping for lunch?"

"If we see somewhere suitable en route." He takes one hand off the wheel and reaches down to undo the zip fly of his trousers. "I'm a little sweaty between the balls right now, but you can chow down on my meat-stick if you like."

I laugh and reach over to zip him back up. "You just concentrate on the road. If you prang Jessica, you're going to be in very deep doo-doo."

"It's all I dream about," he drawls, "being very deep in your doo-doo."

"You've got sex on the brain," I tell him. "I need

174

to source some potassium bromide from somewhere."

"What for?"

"To dampen your ardour, Mackenzie. I can't be on the run with you in this state."

Mackenzie huffs. "I like my ardour exactly the way it is, thanks."

As the sun begins to set we decide to stop at the next place offering accommodation, which happens to be a quaint little *auberge* in a village nestled in a dense forest. It's been a very long day and the bottle of champagne we guzzled this morning is starting to take its toll. All I want to do is fall into bed and go to sleep. I insist on separate rooms, except it turns out there's only one room at the inn. Just my luck! At least it's a twin.

I needn't have worried. Mackenzie doesn't bother me. He's fast asleep the second his head touches the pillow.

We hit the road early the next morning, and by nightfall we're in Munich. Once again we take a twin room, but there couldn't be more of a contrast to where we stayed last night. According to the hotel brochure displayed on the onyx coffee table in our room, Munich was once home to the dukes of Bavaria and now boasts a populace of 1.5 million. All I know is, despite Munich's charm, the place feels alien to me, and the further we drive away from British soil, the more agitated I'm becoming. I never envisaged myself living abroad. I suppose England is in my blood. I can trace my English heritage back to at least the sixteenth century. It's odd, but I have the same feeling that I had after my mum died. I feel like I've been set adrift and I no longer know my place in the world.

I know Mackenzie wouldn't understand, so I keep my thoughts to myself.

Our hotel is in Munich's old town, on the Marienplatz, where the famous Christmas Market is held every year. Our fourth-floor room has a tiny balcony overlooking the elegant square, with just enough room for a couple of cast-iron seats to take in the view. We eat dinner in the hotel's rooftop restaurant, rounding off with a spiced apple dessert called Bavarian Crème, and then Mackenzie orders coffee.

"I did some additional research while you were in the shower," he says, plopping a lump of brown sugar in his cup. "Once we get to Turkey, our options by land are either to drive north through the former Soviet republics or else we have to drive through Syria or Iran."

I grimace. "I don't think any of those choices were ever on my to-do list."

"Me neither, so I did some more digging to see what other options there might possibly be."

"Go home?" I offer, only half joking.

Mackenzie ignores my quip. "I was thinking if we drove down to Turkey's south coast, we might be able to pick up a car ferry straight across the Mediterranean to Egypt. Before all the conflict flared up again in the Middle East, there used to be a ferry service from Turkey to Port Said in Egypt, but it's been suspended indefinitely."

176

"So where does that leave us?"

"Two choices. Either we give up the car..." he pauses for my reaction.

"No," I reply emphatically.

"Or we head down to Italy and see if we can get a car ferry across to Tunisia."

"And then what?"

He shrugs. "It's a pity about the ferry from Turkey. I've always wanted to visit the museum in Cairo, but it's not easy to get to from Tunisia, not unless you want to drive through Libya."

"I'm not sure you're safe around museums," I joke. "I can imagine you walking out with Tutankhamun's mask under your shirt."

Mackenzie laughs. "Maybe you're right. Let's steer clear of museums and art galleries for the time being. Wouldn't want to get tempted."

I pull up a map of Europe on my phone. "Why don't we drive down to Spain, head to Gibraltar, and then hop over to Morocco?"

"Hop over? You make it sound like a doddle. That's a hell of a journey just to get to Gibraltar and then where do we go once we're in Morocco? We're really going to have to ditch the car sooner or later."

"The paintings are locked in the boot. What would we do with those if we got rid of the car?"

"I need to speak to my fence about shifting them. We don't want to be carting them across Europe in the boot of your bloody car. Thing is, after the fiasco with the fake, he's probably not even speaking to me at the moment. We'll have to give it a couple more days and then I'll phone him."

"Who is your fence?" I ask, wondering if he's the same person my dad used to obtain the painting.

"A guy called Lenny the Loot. Why? Does that mean anything to you?"

I shake my head. None of Dad's acquaintances are called Lenny, as far as I know. "Never heard of him. Is he reliable?"

"A hundred percent. I've known him for years."

"So how does it actually work? How do we get paid?"

"Lenny will contact the buyer. Once the buyer has satisfied himself of the authenticity of the piece, he'll be required to deposit the money in a bank account in Siberia."

"Siberia?" I screech.

"It's not *really* in Siberia," Mackenzie assures me. "Nowadays we have to put down false trails so the money can't be traced back to us. We use the same tech that hackers use to bounce the tracer signal around the globe a few times before it ends up in its final destination. It's all gone very high-tech these days. I remember the good old days before the money laundering regs came in. All we had to do was open a numbered bank account in Switzerland or Liechtenstein. It was dead simple."

"I always wanted to own a numbered bank account," I enthuse. "I always thought it sounded really cool."

"You can still open one. You just don't get the anonymity that used to come with it and that makes it useless to a thief."

"So how does it work?"

"The bank allocates you a secret code instead of using your name on the account, but these days it's pointless. The authorities can demand that the bank reveals your true identity. It's a pity. That system used to work really well. It was nice and simple and a whole lot safer than stashing a suitcase full of cash under your mattress."

"And a lot kinder on your back," I point out.

Mackenzie laughs.

"So," I say on a sigh, "what are we supposed to do while we're waiting for Lenny to wire the cash to us?"

Mackenzie shrugs. "Some sightseeing, I guess."

I groan. "I'm homesick already."

"Homesick? You want to go back to Foxwell Manor?"

"No, I meant homesick for England."

"We only left a couple of days ago."

I shrug. "I guess it's in my DNA. I've never been big on travelling."

Mackenzie huffs. "Well, you're going to have to get used to it now we're on the run."

My heart sinks. I'm not sure I'll ever get used to it.

Once we get back to the room, Mackenzie is out like a light. He's been doing all the driving so it's hardly surprising, but I wish I found it so easy to get a peaceful night's sleep. Instead I find myself occupying one of those cast iron seats on the balcony until the small hours, a thousand different thoughts swirling around my head, and not one of them giving me good vibes.

I wake up in need of a pee and notice Aiden's bed is empty. The door to the balcony is slightly ajar and I peek out to see him sat out there, snugly wrapped up in one of the hotel's thick bathrobes.

I take a pee, don the other robe and slippers, and go outside to join him.

"That toilet seat is like a Venus flytrap," I comment, tying the bathrobe belt before taking the vacant seat. "You're standing there, having a pee, and the bloody thing tries to snap shut on you. Lucky I've got good reflexes or the spray would have gone everywhere." He grunts but doesn't reply, which isn't like Aiden. He's always armed with a witty comeback. "What's the matter? Can't sleep?"

He shakes his head. "Too much stuff going through my mind."

"What kind of stuff?"

"You and me kind of stuff."

"Well, it's always hard to sleep when you've got a stiffy."

Aiden throws me a sideways glance. "I wasn't thinking about you in that kind of way."

"You never are. Sometimes I wonder why I stay in this loveless relationship. I shower you with gifts—plastic roses, fake paintings, any little bitty thing your heart desires—and what do I get in return? A threat of incarceration unless I babysit you across Europe."

"I don't know what you've got to complain about. Yesterday morning you threatened to rearrange my entire face."

"Jesus! Have I really gone a whole day without feeling any violent tendencies towards you?"

Aidan narrows his eyes at me. "I never asked you to babysit me across Europe. This was *your* idea."

I shake my head. "No, Aiden. You're the one who insisted we do a road trip because you're so in love with that stupid car of yours."

"Stupid!" Aiden hisses, as if I've insulted him personally.

"Yes and while we're on the subject of your car, I'm curious, why Jessica?"

"If you must know, Frankie gave it that name, after Jessica Rabbit. I suppose because of its curvaceous sex appeal. He used to joke it was too much woman for me to handle."

I can't help but chuckle at that. "Maybe he was right. There's a lot of horsepower beneath those curves."

"Yes, well, I'll say the same to you as I said to him. It may look like it's too hot to handle, but it's really not a dangerous car. It was just drawn to look that way. And if you think my car is stupid, you can get your *thieving arse* out of the driver's seat."

"Okay, it's not a stupid car, but the stupid part is that we're having to travel by road because you can't bear to part with it. And we've got, *not one*, but *two* stolen fucking paintings in the boot of your bright orange DB11. We might as well have a big neon sign over our heads saying 'come and get me.'"

"Be that as it may, it's still *my* car so *I* should drive. Who put you in charge?"

"We could have brought my car on this road trip instead," I argue. "I let you bring yours, so quit complaining."

"That wasn't even your car. It was a hire car and I wouldn't be seen dead in it."

"Well, at least I hired it with my own money. I didn't get my rich daddy to pay for it."

Aiden gasps. "Oh, wow! Are you seriously going to pull *that* card on me every time we argue."

"Look, if it bothers you that much, I'll let you drive tomorrow."

"*Let* me! You see, this is what I'm talking about." Aiden folds his arms across his chest and gazes out across the square, a sulky pout on his lips. "This isn't at all how I envisaged things panning out."

Look," I say in my best conciliatory tone, "it's been a very long day, why don't we talk about this in the morning? Come back to bed. If you're feeling chilly, I'll hop in with you and give you a good warming up."

He huffs. "Not if you're as domineering in bed as you are out of it."

"You know I want you, don't you, Aiden? All this playing hard to get is wearing a bit thin now. Why do humans make such a drama out of a simple act of fucking? Dogs have the right attitude. I wish we were more like them. I could sniff your arse and dry hump you before even saying hello. That's the way sex should be. Uncomplicated and dirty." I glance over at him. "Come on, Aiden. You owe me for double-crossing me. Just a quickie. What do you say?

183

I'm getting a boner just talking about it."

Aiden grunts. "Slip a couple of paracetamols down your throat. That'll take the swelling down."

"Your sympathy is underwhelming. I don't know who you're kidding. You know you want me too."

He unfolds his arms and turns to face me. "Do you still have the shell I gave you?" He makes it sound more like an accusation than a question.

"The good luck charm? Yes I still have it. Why?"

"I was just checking if my gift meant anything to you, or if you tossed it in the bin the second my back was turned."

"No, I was very touched by the gesture."

"Good because that shell has special meaning to me. It's from the very last trip I made to Camber Sands with my mum, so you'd better take good care of it."

"I will," I assure him.

We sit in silence for a few seconds until Aiden speaks up again, his tone softer this time.

"I do like you that way, Mackenzie—I mean sexually—but I'm just not sure that we're reading off the same page yet. I think we should have discussed how this was supposed to end before we started this new chapter."

"Well, it would have helped if I'd had prior warning of your romantic little plan to double-cross me. Personally, I wasn't expecting to ever see you again."

Aiden huffs. "Yes and that wouldn't have bothered you one little bit, would it? You see, this is what I mean. My plans have always included you right from the start, but you were only ever interested in the painting. I never figured in your equation at all, did I?"

"I assumed the two were mutually exclusive. I didn't see how I could steal your inheritance and then expect to have any kind of relationship with you. I'm a thief, Aiden. I did what thieves do. You can't blame me for that. In fact, you positively encouraged it."

"The thing is, Mackenzie, I'm not sure I want to live my life on the run."

"It won't always be this way. As soon as we've cashed in the Raphael we can buy our own private island in the middle of the ocean, where no-one can find us."

He glares at me. "Oh, so that's how you see this panning out, is it? Me and you spending the rest of our days hiding on a remote island? I thought we'd stay in England."

I grunt. "Oh, so you thought we were going to buy some chocolate-box house in the country, with a rose garden and a white picket fence, all wrapped up in a neat little happy-ever-after?"

"No, Mackenzie. I actually had my eye on one of those big beach houses at Camber Sands. You know, the glass-fronted ones with the vaulted ceilings and decking that leads straight onto the dunes. That's the dream. I've always wanted to own one of those."

"Well, I'll tell you what, why don't we pop back to good old Blighty, put the stolen masterpiece down as a deposit on your dream home and hopefully we won't get arrested before we get the deeds."

185

"It's better than your plan. You think we should imprison ourselves on a tiny island in the middle of nowhere."

"Oh, poor Aiden!" I snipe. "Are you worried you might have to spend the rest of your life bumming around in abject luxury in some tropical paradise? Well, I can see why you're losing sleep over that. You must have really deep concerns."

"You can sneer all you like but I'm not a fan of your Robinson Crusoe scenario. That might suit someone *older*, like you, but I don't want to live some place where there's nothing to do."

"Too bad you didn't think of the consequences before you planned this little operation then, isn't it? I thought you were supposed to be the brains of this outfit?"

He gives me a sarcastic smirk. "I am, Mackenzie, and maybe I haven't done thinking this through yet."

"What's that supposed to mean?"

"It means I'm not going back to bed anytime soon." He gets to his feet. "All this talking has made me thirsty. I'm going to raid the mini bar. Do you want something?"

"What are you having?"

"A ginger ale."

"Get me a whisky and ginger, would you?"

"Coming right up."

34 – AIDEN

As we approach the Eurotunnel check-in at Calais I notice Mackenzie's head has slipped down. I lift it back up so it's leaning against the headrest of the passenger seat.

"He's asleep. Long journey," I tell the lady at the check-in kiosk.

She nods and smiles.

"Can we get on the next available single deck carriage. I need low ground clearance for this baby," I say, tapping my steering wheel.

"Yes, certainly."

I hand over my credit card and our passports and a few moments later she passes me a ticket hanger which I slot over my rear view mirror.

Soon we're forty metres beneath the sea bed, hurtling back towards the English coast.

35 – MACKENZIE

The rank smell of stale cooking fat snakes its way up my nostrils, making me feel nauseous and arousing me from my deep slumber. This room smells like I ate a dodgy takeaway in bed last night and then dumped the wrapper on the floor. My cramping stomach concurs with my olfactory sensors. Not only that, I'm so dehydrated my eyelids are glued together and my tongue feels like a cheese grater. I must have had a bloody good session on the booze while I was devouring that nasty food. I try to lift my head but that turns out to be a bad decision.

Oh shit!

I lean over and throw up on the floor.

Ugh!

"Aiden! Water!" I grunt in a scratchy voice. "I need water."

There's no reply. He must be in a similar state to me. With my eyes still closed, I swing my legs out of bed, hoping to set them down somewhere other than where I just threw up. But the floor moves and rustles and my feet sink into it. I can't find solid ground.

What the fuck!

I rub my eyes, trying to encourage my tear ducts to start functioning again. I manage to force my eyelids partially open and then quickly shut them again when a bright light hits my retinas, causing searing pain across my brow. I groan. I feel sick again. I need to get up.

I wiggle my body, trying to slide off the bed, but I can't seem to get out of it. It just rustles and moves, like the floor. I shield my eyes with my hand and try opening them again. What I see makes my brain shoot straight to red alert, overruling the pain in my forehead, and forcing me to sit bolt upright. My heart pounds. I'm certainly fully focused now!

I'm in a rubbish skip, down an alley, next to what smells like a British chippie, and I'm covered in old fish-and-chip wrappers and God knows what else.

How did I...?

And then a faint memory begins to form in the back of my mind. We were in the hotel in Munich. One minute we were chatting and the next minute Aiden was packing our bags, even though it was the middle of the night. I wanted to ask him what he was doing, but I couldn't form the words. It was as if my mouth wasn't connected to my brain. I remember I'd been drinking that night, and what with the exhaustion from all the travelling, it must have sucked all the energy out of me. Then Aiden said we had to go. It was important. And I remember how my heart started racing and I was certain the police must be onto us. We took the lift down to the hotel lobby and I remember Aiden having to help me walk straight because my legs were so shaky. I flopped into the car and that was it. I passed out and woke up here in this skip.

As if I've summoned them up from my imagination, I hear the sound of a police siren and the next thing I know I'm being approached by two uniformed officers, while a third plain-clothes officer stands watching. My heart does a backflip.

"Allow us to help you, sir," one of the uniformed officers says, as he and his colleague assist me out of the skip.

No thief likes being this close to the guardians of law and order. It makes my skin crawl. I try my best to shake off the feeling and act like a normal citizen.

"Thank you so much, officers," I say in a croaky voice. "It's kind of someone to have noticed me in the skip and want to help, but there was really no need to bother the police. I'm sure you've got better things to do than rescue a drunk. I hope you're not going to arrest me for being *drunk and disorderly*. I was at a bachelor party last night, you see, and you know how these things can end up."

"Mackenzie Oden?" the plain-clothes officer bellows, bringing an abrupt halt to my nervous ramblings.

Fuck! He knows my name. "Yes."

He nods at one of the uniformed officers who promptly pulls my hands behind my back. I feel cold metal brush against my wrists, followed by the sound of handcuffs snapping shut.

The plain-clothes officer continues. "I'm arresting you on suspicion of stealing property from Foxwell Manor in Norfolk. You have the right to remain silent and refuse to answer questions, but it may harm your defence if you fail to mention, when questioned, something you later rely on in court. Anything you do say may be used against you in a court of law. You have the right to consult an attorney before speaking to the police and to have an attorney present

191

during questioning. Do you understand your rights, sir?"

I nod, feeling totally numb with shock at this turn of events.

"Aiden," I mumble to myself, as they bundle me into the back of the squad car. "Where's Aiden?" The car sets off and my mind is racing trying to figure out what's going on, and then a horrible thought occurs to me.

This is *his* doing.

I remember when we met up at the Camber Sands hotel after the theft, Aiden threatened to hand me in to the police if I didn't accede to his wishes, and he never wanted to leave England in the first place, so maybe this is his payback.

He must have drugged my drink that night in Munich, when we were chatting on the balcony into the small hours. Presumably he drove us back here and then ditched me in that skip. I can't believe it! Aiden's done it again. He's double-crossed me twice now. Why was I so keen to trust him again after last time? He's been manipulating me from the outset.

Shit! I'm done for. Outsmarted by a twenty-two-year-old. Un-fucking-believable. I must be getting too old for this game. That little shit better hope I never set eyes on him again because I swear I'll kill the conniving bastard with my bare hands.

I'm taken to Folkestone Police Station where I'm again read my rights and told I'm being held for questioning in relation to the art collection at Foxwell Manor, but they don't mention any painting in particular which makes me think they're fishing for information, hoping I'll say something to drop myself in it. I tell them I'm a

192

friend of the family and also an art historian and as such I was invited to view the paintings, but that's all I know. There's no point in pretending Aiden didn't show me the painting because Frankie would be able to testify that much.

They throw me in a cell and then leave me there all night, with thoughts of revenge festering in my brain.

≈

To my amazement, and huge relief, I'm released in the morning without charge. I sign for my valuables and when I get my phone back I discover there's a message waiting for me.

Aiden: *Hi honey! I've reserved a table for lunch. The oysters are to die for. You know where to find me. Bring real roses this time.*

My blood starts to boil. I tap out a quick reply.

Mackenzie: *Hi sweetlips. No roses but I'm bringing a garrotte. It's also to die for.*

I grab a taxi and instruct the cabbie to drop me at The Dunlin hotel in Camber Sands, where Aiden and I met up last time we were on English soil. The journey takes less than an hour but it feels like a year to me, sat on the back seat seething like a man possessed.

Giving a cursory nod to the brunette on reception, I opt for the stairs in preference to the sedate lift. I run up the three flights, assuming Aiden has taken the same room as last time. As I

193

approach Room 30 I can see the door is flung wide open. I pause at the entrance. Standing there in the middle of the room, arms folded in a casual stance, is my double-crossing bestie.

My blood starts to boil again at the sight of him. I enter, slamming the door shut behind me, but I don't immediately close the gap between us. I want to hear what he's got to say before I get within strangling distance.

"Damn, I wish I could have been there," Aiden says with a crooked smile. "I bet you look good in handcuffs."

"You smug bastard," I growl.

Aiden raises his eyebrows. "Ooh, is that your new pet name for me? I think I like it."

"You have approximately two minutes of life left to you so please don't waste it taunting me. I'd like to know precisely what you did to me and why."

"You're out, that's all that matters. Why don't we discuss it over lunch?"

"Was that your idea of a sick joke, having me thrown in jail?"

"Who said it was me?" he asks as if butter wouldn't melt.

I lose my patience and quickly close the gap between us until I'm right up in his face. "That smug message you sent was sort of a clue."

"I only told you where to meet me," he protests.

"You drugged my drink the other night in Munich, didn't you?"

"Might have."

"I knew it. I've been seriously dehydrated ever since I woke up in that skip. My tongue is like a strip of sandpaper. What the hell did you give me?"

"A Mickey Finn."

"A Mickey Finn!" I scoff. "Who the hell do you think you are, some kind of gangster?"

"Well, I think that's what they used to call it in those old espionage thrillers."

"You *think*? You're shoving chemicals down my throat and you don't even know what they are? What are you trying to do, kill me?"

He sighs and rolls his eyes, as if he's bored with this conversation already. "I know exactly what it is. Chloral hydrate."

"Isn't that a date rape drug?"

Aiden's lip curls. "Mackenzie, *pleeease!* You don't need any coercion. I could have had you anytime I wanted. I'm not surprised you're dehydrated, the way you've been drooling over me since the day we met."

"I should have punched you in the face the last time you double-crossed me. You got away with it once, so you've done it again. It's my fault. I've gone soft in the head."

"You're making a fuss over nothing. My mum used to take chloral hydrate to help her sleep. It's a sedative that used to be commonly prescribed by doctors. It's perfectly safe."

"Yeah, if you know what you're doing, rather than some kid playing with someone else's life."

"I'm not a kid."

"Where did you get it? Don't tell me you found some of your mother's old supplies in the bathroom cabinet."

"No. I bought it online. From Bulgaria."

195

"You spiked my drink with some dodgy drug you bought online?"

"It's not dodgy. I tried it on myself first. Admittedly, not as much as I had to give you, but I had no ill effects."

"What were you even doing with it in the first place?"

Aiden shrugs. "Experimenting. I told you, I'm into all that spy shit."

"And you thought you'd bring some along on our trip, did you?"

"Well, I do like to have my little insurance policies, just in case things don't go as planned."

"How long was I out for?"

His cheeks flush and he looks away. "Not long."

"How long?" I insist.

"A couple of days."

"Days!"

"It was a long drive back. When you started coming to, I had to give you spiked water to knock you out again."

I glare at him, my teeth grinding. "Weren't you even a tiny bit afraid of what I might do to you when I got here? Because if this is your idea of foreplay, I can only assume you like it rough." I pause for a moment as my brain throws up an odd question that requires an answer. "How did you manage to lift me into that skip? You couldn't have done it on your own."

"A homeless man helped me. I bought him fish and chips."

"Aww, Aiden, that's nice!" I drawl sarcastically. "It's a bit like when one of those charity bags gets

196

shoved through your letterbox asking for any unwanted items. It's always nice to combine getting rid of your junk with helping out someone less fortunate than yourself."

"I chose that place very carefully," he protests. "You looked nice and comfy in there when I left. Anyway, it's all your fault. If you'd have listened to my genuine concerns, none of this would have happened, but I knew I was wasting my breath."

"Do you know what your problem is, Aiden? You're too used to getting your own way. Someone really needs to teach you some humility. You double-crossed me and then blackmailed me and now you've drugged me and double crossed me again. What's next?"

He shrugs. "The day is young, Mackenzie. You'd better be nice to me."

I watch as his demeanour changes and his shoulders slump.

"Look, Mackenzie, I don't want to argue with you. Can we just agree to start over? I have a surprise for you." He turns and points to the far wall, to a sofa where the two paintings are sitting side by side. I gasp and move forward to take a closer look.

"Wow! You can really tell the difference when they're together like this."

"I know," Aiden says coming to stand beside me. "That's why I got them out for you. I thought you'd be interested. They make a pretty pair, don't they?" He loops his arm into mine. "Just like me and you."

I twist my head to give him a glacial stare. "Don't push your luck."

Aiden wisely pulls his arm free.

I turn my attention back to the paintings, my heart enthused by the sight of them. "You don't really notice when you view each one separately, but it's obvious when you see them like this that the real one has a more varied palette. It's funny because all the images of this painting online actually represent the fake more faithfully than the real one. And I suppose, thinking about it, that makes sense. The thing is until now, no-one in living memory has seen the real painting to be able to faithfully reproduce the image online. The only thing we had to go on was black-and-white photographs and the fake."

"But I've seen colour photographs of it online," Aiden insists.

"Yes, but the colour has been artificially applied to a black-and-white photograph to give an impression of what the real thing might look like."

"Well if the fake was painted in the seventeenth century, you would assume the artist had actually seen the original, so why didn't he use the exact same shades?"

I nod. "Good question. Cost probably. Unknown artist. Penniless amateur. He had all the talent but not the money to faithfully reproduce it. The most neutral-coloured pigments were a lot cheaper. The other shades, like the greens and the blues, probably even the synthesised vermillion, all had to be imported."

"I was afraid you might spot the difference when I switched the paintings," Aiden admits. "I know the differences are just in colour tone, but you *had* just examined the original close up."

"I was too focused on the security sensors on

the wall." I turn to face him head on. "What's to stop me taking the original right now and walking out of the door with it?"

"You wouldn't do that to me, Mackenzie, not when I just saved your arse."

"Saved my arse! How do you figure that?"

"That's why I had you arrested, so we wouldn't have to be on the run anymore. That wasn't the life for us, hiding away in some foreign country. You'll see. You'll thank me for it one day."

I fold my arms across my chest and gaze at him pointedly. "I'm confused. You want me to thank you...for having me arrested? Explain that to me."

"I spoke to Frankie and admitted to taking the fake painting. I said I was doing a grand tour of Europe and I needed money to fund my trip. I knew my dad wouldn't be too worried about me taking the copy because it was just sat in storage. Sure, he'll be annoyed that I didn't ask, but it might as well be used for something useful, like funding my much-needed education in life, rather than sitting in storage. Besides, he's on a luxury tour of Canada with his girlfriend, spending my inheritance, so why shouldn't I be doing the same?"

"Okay, so you spoke to Frankie, and then what?"

"Then I phoned Folkestone Police to give them an anonymous tip-off that a painting had gone missing from Foxwell Manor and a man who knew the family, and could be implicated, was currently sleeping off a hangover in a skip in Landon Alley. After they arrested you on suspicion, they phoned the manor, got through to Frankie and he told them it was a misunderstanding and that I had taken a painting and sold it to fund a trip. They then got in touch with me to verify the story. So you see I just did you a massive favour."

I unfold my arms and drag a hand through my hair, feeling utterly perplexed. Once again Aiden is running rings around me and I'm playing catch up. "You did *me* a favour?"

"Yes, don't you see? You're off the hook now. The police have already looked into the so-called missing painting and found you to be innocent. And as everyone knows, a person can't be arrested twice for the same crime."

"Of course they bloody can," I scoff. "Double jeopardy only applies if the case actually goes to court and the defendant is acquitted."

"Oh! Is that so? Well, I'm not a thief, so I'm no expert in being arrested. I was just going on what I'd heard."

"Do you really expect me to fall for that load of bollocks? You're smarter than that, Aiden. You had me arrested for *one* reason and I'll tell you exactly what it is. It's because of the disagreement we had over where to live, isn't it? You wanted to prove a point, that you can have me arrested any damn time you like so I'd better toe the line. You see, I've figured out how your mind works, Aiden Foxwell. I bet you're still holding onto that security camera footage as well, aren't you?"

He shrugs. "I told you it's my insurance policy. Why would I get rid of it?"

"Don't forget, you're not so innocent yourself. You aided and abetted me, so before you think of turning me over to the police again, bear that in mind because I can promise you, if you pull that stunt on me again, you'll very quickly find yourself in the next cell."

"So much aggression, Mackenzie! You really must learn to chill. Stress can kill you."

"Is there any wonder I'm stressed after what I've been through? Do you know what, Aiden, I really don't know where we go from here because there's no way there can ever be any trust between us after what you've just done."

"You can trust me, honey," Aiden purrs. "All you have to do is play nice and we'll get on just fine."

"And by 'play nice' you mean tug my forelock every time you speak and agree with everything you say. Yeah, right! This isn't Foxwell bloody Manor. This is the real world. Not everything in life goes according to the Gospel of St. Aiden. What you need is someone to bring you down a peg or two." Just in that precise moment an unbidden thought pops into my head—a crazy idea that sets my head spinning. "No, no, no. That is diabolical. Absolutely not. No way!"

Aiden scowls at me. "What?"

I start laughing. A crazy sort of teary-eyed laugh. I swear some of Aiden's insanity has rubbed off on me.

"Come on, Mackenzie, let me in on the joke. What are you laughing at?"

"It's just occurred to me that there's only *one* way I can be certain you'll never hand me over to the police again. I hate it, but it's totally logical, and you can't argue with logic."

Aiden's eyes widen. "You're going to kill me?"

I huff. "Okay, you're right, there are *two* ways to stop you ever fucking me over again. But no, Aiden, I'm not going to kill you. I'm going to marry you."

Aiden stares at me slack-jawed.

I rub the tears of laughter from my eyes. "Don't look at me like that. It's what you envisaged when you planned this whole thing, isn't it? Me and you, riding off into the sunset together, with our happy-ever-after waiting for us on the horizon."

"Married?" he repeats, his face drained of colour. "Me and you?" He shakes his head. "We're only just getting properly acquainted. I'm not even sure you really like me that much."

"What's that got to do with anything? I'm afraid it's the only way if we're to remain as partners in this venture. You see, Aiden, you can't testify against your spouse, so you can forget about trying to blackmail me with that stupid security footage once we're married."

"Is this a joke?"

"Oh no. I'm deadly serious. I want my half of the proceeds and you need someone to hold your hand and show you how to do the whole adulting thing."

"Fuck you, Mackenzie. Why can't you just admit this is about more than the painting? You know you have feelings for me but you're too afraid of your own emotions to admit it."

"No, I'm afraid of you double-crossing me at every turn."

"And your answer is to force me to marry you?" he replies incredulously.

"No-one's forcing you, Aiden. It's entirely your

choice." I nod towards the exit. "I can walk out of that door now, but I'll be taking the painting with me and I'll take my chances that you won't hand me in because you're implicated too and I've already told you what will happen."

He thrusts his chin at me. "My dad would get me out."

"Don't count on it. Are you going to marry me or not? You have exactly five seconds to make up your mind."

"You're even crazier than I am and that's saying something."

"Three seconds."

"Seriously, Mackenzie, that has got to be the worst marriage proposal in the history of the universe."

"One second."

"Why can't we discuss this like grown-ups?"

"Time's up, What's it to be?"

He glares at me. "Fuck! You'd better buy me real roses, Mackenzie. Lots of them."

I laugh. "It hurts, doesn't it?"

"What does?"

"Being outsmarted."

"You should know," he grunts.

"No roses, Aiden. You've been a naughty boy, getting me thrown in jail. I'll be buying you a ring and that's all you're getting." I lean in so my nose almost touches his. "And bear this in mind. If we go through with this arrangement, I shall expect to partake of my conjugal rights the second we're married. You're supposed to be my inside man and I haven't been inside you once yet."

"Very funny. What's the matter, Mackenzie, are you getting a stiffy just thinking about being married to me?"

"If I had a stiffy there'd be more of a gap between us than this."

He huffs. "You realise you're going to have to live up to this image you're painting, don't you?"

"You're right, it's not wise for a man to brag about the size of his assets before the big reveal, but then I'm not convinced you've even seen a real man's dick in the flesh before. Those tiddlers you played with at boarding school don't count."

"So you think you're on safe ground because I have nothing to compare yours to? Think again. My last boyfriend called his dick Rottie. Short for Rottweiler."

"How amusing. I call mine Badger because it's got a wide, stumpy body; it's mostly nocturnal; and it likes nothing more than burrowing into dark holes."

Aiden's lip sneers. "And does it also have a disgusting odour?"

"I think you're getting mixed up with a skunk."

"Oh yes! Sorry about that," he says with a sarcastic grin.

"I don't think you're sorry at all. *About anything.* Including having me thrown in jail."

He reaches out and fiddles with a button on my shirt, making my dick jump to immediate attention. "No, I'm not sorry about that. I think it's wise to keep you on your toes, Mackenzie."

I put my arms around him and pull him tight to me, so our bodies are moulded as one. He gazes up at me and I can tell by the smouldering look in his eyes that he can feel my bulge digging into his hip. "You listen to me, Aiden Foxwell. There are going to be a few changes in this relationship once we're married, so don't say I didn't warn you."

"There's more chance of aliens landing than you being boss of me, Mackenzie, so dream on."

I press my lips to his and he treats me to a kiss more intense, more passionate, than anything we've ever shared before. If I'm not mistaken, he's turned on by the idea of marriage. I must confess I, too, am totally enamoured with the idea of sharing the marital bed with my duplicitous little bestie.

36 – AIDEN

I can't believe it. After Mackenzie's marriage proposal—was it a proposal or a threat? It's hard to tell with him—we flew straight out to Vegas, bought ourselves a wedding licence and got married in one of those cheesy chapels on the Strip. It wasn't the most romantic fifteen minutes of my life—more like a shotgun wedding really, on account of Mackenzie insisting on such a hastily-arranged ceremony—but I'm not complaining. Even when Mackenzie thinks he's the boss of me, I still manage to get exactly what I want. I think this is going to work out just great. It's no real hardship for me to be married to my worldly-wise gentleman thief. I like a man who knows how to take care of me and show me a good time. Finally I'm free of the shackles of my upbringing, ready to live my own life without being weighed down by expectation and responsibility.

It's been a sort of whirlwind romance, but without the romance. I think Mackenzie put a spell on me, or maybe I put one on him. Our 'courtship' has been a swashbuckling adventure filled with lies, deceit, skulduggery and mayhem. I've loved every second of it. And now look at me. I'm a married man.

This is going to shock a lot of people back home when they find out. I can just see the headline in the gossip magazines.

"Heir to Foxwell Manor elopes to Sin City with his gay lover for a quickie Vegas wedding."

Oh my God! I haven't even told my dad we're an item yet. I don't know which he's going to kill me for first—arranging the theft of his Raphael or marrying the man who stole it.

We don't even have to go anywhere for our honeymoon, not with a million casinos, bars, live shows, cinemas and restaurants right on our doorstep. Not that we really have time for a proper honeymoon. We fly home tomorrow because we left the two paintings locked in the boot of my car in the hotel car park in Camber Sands. We daren't leave them there too long, but I'm trying my best not to think about that right now. It's not every day a boy meets a man from right out of his fantasies and ends up marrying him.

My new full name is Aiden Somerton Foxwell-Oden. Yes, I'm officially a real mouthful!

We're celebrating in the hotel lounge with a couple of Honeymooner cocktails before heading back up to our top-floor suite. At least that's what I thought we were doing. But Mackenzie has other ideas en route...

37 – MACKENZIE

Well, I never thought I'd see the day, but here I am, a married man. After celebrating with a couple of cocktails in the bar, Aiden and I decide to head on up to our hotel suite. We opt for one of the gleaming *glass-bottomed elevators*, as opposed to one of the traditional lifts favoured by the more squeamish guests. It's not even that scary because it's not as if it's one of those lifts that runs up the outside of the building. All you can see when you look down is the elevator shaft, although to be fair it's nicely lit up with different coloured lights, so it gives the impression of travelling through a wormhole in space.

The rear wall of the lift is mirrored and as we enter I can't help but notice what a dapper couple we make in our matching turquoise tuxedos. Amid the strains of orchestral music coming from the tinny speakers, Aiden hits the button marked 31 and we wait to be whisked to the top floor. Nothing happens for several seconds but thankfully no-one else joins us and the doors finally close. I'm glad we're alone because I've been dreaming of this moment ever since we first met.

Being a thief, I've spent a fair amount of my life going up and down lifts in impressive buildings and I've discovered something perhaps not widely known by the general public. These lifts usually have a discreet service button, marked with a spanner icon, that's set apart from the other buttons so it doesn't get accidently hit. It's intended for the sole use of the maintenance people, to take the lift out of commission for five or ten minutes or however long they've pre-programmed it for. During a meticulously planned robbery, this button can come in very handy when you're trying to hog the lift and time the exact moment it arrives at a different floor. Unlike pressing the big red *Stop* button, this doesn't set any alarm bells ringing in the controller's office.

As soon as the lift gets moving I hit the service button and the lift comes to an immediate halt. I spin Aiden around so he has his back to me, and then I grab him by the waist and lift him up in the air. "Flip that security camera around so it's facing the side wall," I tell him.

"What for?"

"Just do it," I grunt, my biceps straining.

He adjusts the camera so we have some privacy and then I set him back down and scoot up behind him, wrapping my arms around him.

"What are you up to?" Aiden asks.

"This."

He watches in the mirror as I flip open the top button of his trousers, a soft smirk spreading across his lips before he pushes my hand away.

"Patience, Mackenzie."

"I've been very patient," I whisper in his ear as I plant a row of kisses down the nape of his neck.

"That tickles," he sighs, arching his back and turning his head to the side so I can kiss his parted lips. I flick my tongue inside his mouth, tasting the fruity cocktail flavours still lingering there, and then I grab the tab on his zip and begin to slowly ease it down. He gasps and spins around to face me.

"Seriously? You want to do it right here in the lift? Surely you can wait until we get to our room, you frisky old coot."

"I could," I say breathlessly, "but this is way more fun."

He shakes his head. "I'm not doing it in a lift. This is our wedding day. Show some respect."

I'm draped all over him, groping his arse, unable to keep my hands off him. "I'll respect you in the morning. Get undressed and let's fuck!" I growl.

"I bet you don't even have any lube on you," he whines.

"I'm afraid not. A bit of spit will have to suffice."

"Won't you find that painful?"

I let go of him and take a step back. "Me?"

He nods. "I usually top."

"No, I top," I insist.

Aiden bursts out laughing. "I'm just kidding with you. You really haven't worked out the difference between my serious face and my teasing face yet have you?"

"Oh so you're admitting you're two-faced. Well, my love, how can I tell them apart when I'm dazzled by your beauty. Both of your faces look hideously attractive to me."

"Why am I never sure whether you're complementing me or insulting me?"

"Because I like you confused. It helps me keep one step ahead."

"Get real, Mackenzie. You know you're always playing catch up. I like to keep you on your toes. You can't run when you're on your toes."

"Run? Why would I want to run? I like it right where I am. Here, alone in this lift with you, with a serious boner in my pants, which by the way needs immediate attention before it explodes in situ."

"Okay, look, if you really can't wait I'll give it a quick suck, but that's it."

I screw my nose up. "A quick suck?"

"Take it or leave it."

"How romantic!" I grumble as I unzip my fly. "I wait all this time and what am I getting? A quick suck."

Aiden plucks the silk handkerchief from his chest pocket and bends over to waft it over the floor of the lift, giving it a light dusting. He shoves the handkerchief back in his pocket before sinking to his knees. When he looks up at me with those big brown puppy-dog eyes of his, I feel my dick fidgeting impatiently in my underwear. I release it from its confines and Aiden switches his gaze from me to it.

"Shit!" he gasps. "You weren't lying. It *is* thick and stumpy. How am I supposed to fit that in my mouth without gagging? I'd need a throat like the Grand Canyon."

"Well, you have a big enough mouth the rest of the time, so I'm sure you'll manage." I hold it at the root and angle it towards his mouth.

"So I've got a big mouth and I'm two-faced? You keep paying me those kinds of compliments and you might end up with some teeth marks in your dick."

"More than your life is worth," I assure him. "Now, shut up and suck."

"Just don't dribble down my Zegna."

"If I dribble down your suit it will be your fault. If you lick, suck and swallow, like a good boy, you shouldn't spill a drop."

"Oh, you expect me to swallow!" His tone is a mix of incredulity and amusement. "And how long exactly have you been storing it in there?" he prods my ballsack making me flinch. "You've had a permanent hard-on since the day we met. I hope you've given it a good tug recently."

I sigh. *Like that's anyone's business but my own.* "You really know how to kill the moment, don't you? For your information, I had a bloody good wank in the shower this morning. My current load couldn't be any fresher. Happy?"

"Ecstatic. I'm very particular about consuming stuff by its use-by date."

I clasp my hand around the back of his head and hold him in place while I press my bulbous glans to his lips. "Now get on with it."

"Wait," he says, his hands pushing against my hips. "Show me how hairy it is and I'll let you know if I still fancy it."

"I've got news for you, we're married. Whether you *fancy it* or not, you're stuck with it. That's what you get for not taking it out for a test drive."

"Come on, let me see."

I grumble to myself as I tug my trousers and underwear lower, so they're resting half way down my thighs.

He eyes my groin. "Okay, it's not gross. Some

older men don't bother grooming at all. I don't want to choke on a load of bindweed while I'm down there, but yours is quite neat."

"I'm delighted it passes muster, Your Lordship. Now, if you don't get the hell on with it your bloody Zegna suit is going to get a christening from my font."

"Okay but you have to press the button first."

"What?"

"You wanted it to be fun. It'll be more exciting if it's time-limited. I'm giving you until we reach the top floor and then you have to zip yourself back up and put it away until tonight."

"You bastard!" I complain.

"I thought we'd agreed on *smug* bastard."

"You're right, you smug bastard."

I tilt my dick towards his mouth again. "Press it now, Mackenzie."

I hammer the service button and we set off again, hurtling towards the top floor at a rate of knots and then I feel Aiden's warm mouth wrapping around my hard-on. My stomach twists and it feels like I'm soaring through space at warp speed. I look down to see his head jigging up and down, and beneath him the wormhole effect of coloured lights streaking by. It's a weird sight and combined with the sensation of Aiden's intense oral ministrations, I start to feel lightheaded. I brace myself against the lift wall.

"Oh fuck, yes!" I moan, glancing up at the digital display. *15, 16, 17.* "That's it, keep going," I pant, feeling sweat breaking out across my brow. Then a sudden thought occurs to me, causing momentary panic. "What if someone calls the lift before we reach the top?"

Aiden mumbles something in response but I can't understand a word of it on account of his mouth being stuffed full of my throbbing erection.

"That's so fucking good!" I grunt through gritted teeth as Aiden uses both his hand and mouth to drive me right to the edge. I check the display again. The floors are racing by. *21, 22, 23.*

"Oh shit, I'm coming. I'm coming now!" I feel the hot surge rise up and shoot forth into Aiden's throat. Fortunately for him, my climax is short-lived due to me having already relieved myself once this morning. When I've finished emptying my load I glance up to see we've almost reached our floor. *28, 29, 30.* "Stick your tongue out," I tell him. *...and 31.* There's a *ping* and then the lift doors open just as I'm slapping my dick against Aiden's outstretched tongue to knock the last few drops out. He finishes off by giving me one last suck to wash it clean. It's amazing how obedient and attentive he is when you give him something to play with. I roll my head back and sigh. "That was awesome."

It's then I notice something in my peripheral vision. I twist my head around and standing there, waiting to enter the lift, is an elderly couple, gawking at us in stunned silence.

"Fuck!" I mutter as I pluck my spent dick out of Aiden's mouth and quickly pull my trousers back up.

"Mmm...," he moans, smacking his lips. "Fresh is best. Tastes like salted caramel."

"Get up," I grunt under my breath. It's only then he spots the old man and woman. He jumps to his feet, wiping his mouth with the back of his hand.

"I, er, I lost the button off my suit trousers," I explain in a slightly hysterical-sounding voice. "This young man was just helping me look for it."

"Aww, isn't that sweet of him," the old lady gushes with a mawkish smile. "It's nice to know that kindness still exists even in today's world. And look at that. You've even got matching suits. Isn't that a coincidence!"

Her husband gives me a filthy look and then puts his arm around his wife's shoulder and leads her away. "Come on, Mavis, we'll take a different elevator."

38 – AIDEN

My mouth drops open when we enter our hotel suite. In the ninety minutes or so since we were last in our room, someone's added three vases full of long-stem red roses and there's a magnum of champagne sitting on the coffee table.

I turn to Mackenzie. "Oh my God, this is amazing. Did you arrange this?"

A rare flush of embarrassment tinges Mackenzie's cheeks. "I had a mad moment of feeling romantic but it quickly passed. However, I'd already ordered all this by then, so I guess we're stuck with it."

"I love it." I turn and plant a kiss on his lips.

"I'm not sure what it is with you and roses, but I thought you'd like them."

"My mum loved roses. I always used to buy her a bunch on her birthday. They made her face light up and now that's how they make me feel inside. I smile every time I see a rose."

Mackenzie looks at me and grimaces. "It's more like a demented grin than a smile. If you don't wipe that look off your face you're liable to end the day in a straight jacket."

I laugh. "What use would I be to you in a straight jacket on our wedding night?"

"Oh, I don't know, Aiden," Mackenzie drawls. "I'd kind of like to have you bound and gagged on our wedding night."

"Don't go getting any kinky ideas. I'm not that

kind of boy."

"Bloody hell. I suppose I'll just have to settle for fucking your brains out then."

"Don't go thinking the champagne and roses buy you a free pass. I'm not a done deal, Mackenzie."

"I'm not worried. I've got the rest of the day to charm the pants off you. You're mine tonight, Aiden Foxwell-Oden. You can count on it."

"Only if you ply me with enough alcohol," I tease.

"Coming right up!" Mackenzie pops the champagne cork and fills the two flutes with frothy fizz.

The rest of the afternoon is spent imbibing and chatting in the whirlpool bathtub, and then we dress and head out for a night on the town. Strolling arm-in-arm, we make our way up the Strip with expectations of walking from one end to the other, not realising how long it actually is. We call into a couple of casinos to play the slots, but after only making it about a quarter of the way up the Strip, we turn around and head back to our hotel for dinner.

We choose to eat in the atrium restaurant by the fountain and as we sit chatting away, it dawns on me that we've been talking non-stop all day. Normally, I get bored very quickly conversing with people, but he and I seem to be on the same wavelength. Being in his company feels like the most natural thing in the world to me. I find it hard to imagine how dull my life must have been before we met. *Is this how everyone feels on their wedding night?* I wonder.

Mackenzie gazes at me across the table,

candlelight flickering in his blue-grey eyes. "When I was in that cell in Folkestone, I honestly had visions of wrapping my hands around your throat and strangling every last breath out of you. And now look at us."

"You had to wait to be thrown into prison before you got those feelings? How weird!" I jibe. "I felt that way about you from the second you bid on me at that auction."

Mackenzie chuckles. "Yeah, I didn't know you could still buy a bride at auction."

I flick a pea at him. "I didn't realise how easy it is to entrap a thief."

He flicks one of his own peas back at me. "Aiden, can we be serious for just one second?"

"If we must."

"I'm curious. When did your feelings for me change? Was there a specific moment?"

I mull it over for a few seconds. "I'm not sure exactly. It was a bit like that Stockholm syndrome."

"What are you talking about? I didn't hold you captive."

"But you did involve me in a crime. You used the fact I'm gay to get close to me so you could get access to the painting."

"I had dinner with you a couple of times. Where's the harm? I didn't make you do anything against your will."

"Except marry you," I tease.

Mackenzie smiles. "You don't look like you're struggling with the concept of being married to me."

"No, but I still struggle with the fact that once

you had the painting safely tucked under your arm, you tried to walk out of my life without even a backward glance. If I hadn't switched the paintings, we wouldn't be where we are right now. Was I really just collateral damage as far as you were concerned?"

"You were *supposed* to be, but I didn't reckon on you being so...so you. I don't know what it is about you, Aiden, but you managed to squirm your way under my skin. I did try to walk away, except I couldn't stop thinking about you. I know this is going to sound daft, but that old Lionel Richie song—*Stuck on You*—kept playing in my head."

"Stuck? You mean like stale chewing gum on the bottom of your shoe?"

"Yes, exactly that. And I haven't been able to shake you off since."

The waiter swoops in to clear our plates away. "Would you gentlemen like to see the dessert menu?"

"I don't need a menu," I reply eagerly. "I'd like ice-cream, please."

"Certainly. What flavour would you like?"

I gaze straight into Mackenzie's eyes as I reply to the waiter. "Salted caramel. My husband gave me a mouthful of his this morning and I was so overawed by it I couldn't speak."

The waiter taps my order into his tablet device. "Coming right up."

I kick Mackenzie under the table. "Isn't that what you said when you shoved it in my mouth. '*Coming right up*' or words to that effect."

Mackenzie glares back at me for a second before turning his attention to the waiter. "I'll just have a brandy, thanks."

"Very good, sir."

When the waiter's gone, Mackenzie grins at me. "Don't gorge yourself on that ice-cream, I'm on a promise tonight and I've already whipped up a fresh batch of salted caramel for you."

"Well, you haven't tasted mine yet," I point out.

The ice-cream arrives promptly and it's a matter of mere moments for me to polish it off. A moment on the lips, a lifetime on the hips—isn't that what they say? I've never wined and dined so much as I have since I met Mackenzie. Unless my dad was at home, I just used to snack, rather than eat proper meals. I think I might have to start watching my weight if we carry on like this.

Mackenzie decides he wants to have a smoke while he's finishing off his brandy, so we adjourn to the palm-treed garden. We find a wooden seat that's vacant and Mackenzie lights up his cigar.

"I don't mind the smell of cigars," I tell him. "Not a fan of cigarettes, but cigars remind me of my great-uncle. He never married, so he used to come over for Christmas dinner every year and he'd always end the meal with a brandy and cigar."

Mackenzie takes another puff before replying. "I only treat myself to a smoke on special occasions. I think getting married counts as one of those."

Just then my phone rings and when I check who's calling my heart almost jumps out of my chest. I stare at Mackenzie. "It's my dad."

"Well, I think you'd better pick up then, don't you?" Mackenzie suggests.

"I know but...what am I going to say to him?"

Mackenzie shrugs. "You're supposed to be the brains of the operation."

"Oh that was helpful," I sneer as I accept the call and press the phone to my ear. "Hi Dad!" I say in an overly cheery voice. "How's Canada?"

Dad's sombre voice rumbles against my eardrum. "I think we need to talk, my boy."

I stand and begin pacing back and forth in front of Mackenzie, shoving my free hand in my pocket. "Something wrong, Dad?" I ask, giving Mackenzie a vexed expression.

"Where the hell are you? I leave you on your own for five minutes—"

"No, not five minutes, Dad. You told me you'd be gone for a couple of months."

"Well, Canada's a big place."

"Yeah and so is the rest of the world and I want to see some of it."

"Frankie told me you're doing a tour of Europe. Are you with that Mackenzie person?"

"Yes, I'm with Mackenzie."

"And there's something else we need to discuss, isn't there? Missing artwork, for example."

"I already explained that to Frankie. I needed some way to fund my trip and it was only stuck in storage."

"*Both* of them, Aiden. We need to talk about *both* missing items."

"Oh, shit!" I stop pacing and make a face at Mackenzie.

"What's wrong?" Mackenzie asks. I shake my head, not wishing to discuss it while my dad is still on the line.

222

"Get your arse back home pronto, young man, or there will be consequences. Do I make myself clear?"

"Yes, Dad."

"And bring that Mackenzie person with you."

"Are you back in England?"

"Yes I am, Aiden, thanks to you. Don't keep me waiting long. I'll expect to hear back from you in a couple of days." He ends the call and, somewhat dazed, I slip the phone back into my pocket.

Mackenzie scowls at me. "What did he say?"

I retake my seat, wringing my hands as I speak. "He knows about the Raphael."

Mackenzie groans. "What? How? Oh fuck! I thought you said..."

"Yeah, I know what I said, so let's not start with the blame game already."

"Well, what's he going to do about it?"

"I've no idea. All I know is he's requested our presence back at the manor house. Pronto."

"Both of us?"

"Yes. And when I say *requested*, I actually mean he *commanded* our presence."

"I guess it's lucky we're flying home tomorrow then, isn't it?"

I twist to face Mackenzie. "What do you think this means?"

He shrugs. "If he was going to call the police he would have done it by now. Obviously he doesn't want the family name dragged through the dirt."

"But what about the Raphael?"

"He can't force us to give it back. It's not as if

he obtained it legally himself, so he's really got no grounds to stand on."

"Why do you think he wants to see us then?"

"Probably wants to persuade you not to run off with me, but to stay and marry some nice girl instead. He might even be planning on using the painting as a bargaining chip to buy me off or something."

"Wow, your mind is almost as devious as mine, Mackenzie. If that's his plan, he's going to get a bit of a shock when I tell him we're married."

Mackenzie chuckles. "Isn't he just!"

A sudden thought crosses my mind and twists into my gut like a knife. "You're not going to let him buy you off, are you?"

He huffs. "Don't be ridiculous. What could he give me that I don't already have?"

"That's true. So everything's going to be okay?"

"Of course," he assures me. "I'll tell you something else. I'm not going to let this ruin our wedding night. If we have to fly home tomorrow and face the music, so be it. But until then, Mr. Aiden Foxwell-Oden, you're all mine."

39 – MACKENZIE

I'm not worried about the phone call from Aiden's father. Whatever he's got to say to us, I'm confident it doesn't involve having either of us arrested. He daren't involve the police since he has no legal claim to either painting himself, having obtained them on the black market. He must have also surmised that Aiden's implicated, not only in the theft of the fake but of the Raphael too. Basically, Lord Foxwell can shout and rant all he wants but he has no ammunition he can use against us. There's no point him demanding pistols at dawn if he can only fire blanks. Aiden and I have nothing to be concerned about. Tonight is our wedding night and I won't allow that phone call from Lord Foxwell to ruin it.

After I finish my brandy, we make our way back up to our hotel suite and slump on the sofa. Aiden shuffles up to me and rests his head on my shoulder. I twist my head to kiss him, but it cricks my neck so I ask him to stand while I stretch my legs out along the full length of the sofa. I pat my thigh, inviting him to sit there. "Come here and give your husband a kiss."

He grins at me. "I like that. My husband. That's going to take a bit of getting used to." He climbs onto my lap, his legs straddling my thighs, and I wrap my hand around the back of his neck and pull him in for a slow, tender kiss. And yet I sense hesitancy in him and when he pulls away his eyes are cast down, as if he's nervous or anxious about something.

"Mackenzie."

"Yes?"

"I need to ask you something."

"What?"

"I know the way we ended up together isn't exactly conventional but...we're still a real couple, aren't we?"

I shoot back a flippant response, not really in the mood for conversation. "Well I should bloody well hope so after I married you this morning."

Now he looks me in the eyes, a scowl marring his brow. "But what I mean is, you won't ever cheat on me, will you? Not even with a woman."

Oh, so that's what's bothering him. "Aiden, maybe when we first met I shouldn't have bragged about my past conquests in that cavalier fashion but you have to forget all that now. You've flipped my world on its head. Everything is going to be different from now on." I raise my left hand and waggle my ring finger at him. "See this? I've never been a fan of jewellery but this ring is different. It's special because you gave it to me when we made our vows. It symbolises that we're a team now and no-one can come between us."

"Yes, I know we're a team, but is this just a business arrangement? I mean, you said you were only marrying me because—"

"So that you could never testify against me," I interrupt. "Yes. I know what I said."

"Well?"

"Well, after what happened in Folkestone that was definitely an issue that needed addressing.

Who knows what your next trick will be? You're always saying you like to keep me on my toes and this is my way of making sure your little games don't get out of hand again, like they did last time. But let's get real, Aiden. I wouldn't have married you if I hated your guts."

He makes jazz hands at me. "Ooh, lucky me! My husband doesn't hate my guts. Maybe I'll have that printed on a t-shirt."

I snort. "Yes and on the back you can print *But the day is young.* I'm sure you won't be able to stay out of mischief for long. It's like a drug to you, isn't it? After all, it must be two days since you last made me want to kill you so I expect you're getting withdrawal symptoms. I know you like nothing better than finding ways to make my blood boil."

He stares blankly at me, unamused.

"Look, all I'm trying to say is that you're different. I've never met anyone like you before."

"Like me?"

"Someone who thinks blackmail is a form of foreplay."

Aiden remains stony-faced.

"Hand on heart, Aiden, I can't think of a single other person in the world that I'd be willing to marry just to stop them double-crossing me on an almost daily basis, so you'll have to draw your own conclusions from that."

"I conclude that no-one else you've met has ever double-crossed you."

"That is true."

"So then I have no-one else to compare myself to in the hierarchy of your affections."

"I don't do affection. I don't do relationships. And I definitely don't do marriage. So you can see that all this is as baffling to me as it is to you. I've no idea how we ended up here in such a short space of time, but people like you and I don't follow normal protocols. We're rule breakers. We don't act like normal people. We do what our gut tells us to do. We trust our instincts."

Aiden heaves a deep sigh, his face contorted as if a dog chewed it up and spat it out. "The thing is, Mackenzie, I really need to know how you feel about me because...I hate to say it but...I think I might be falling for you in a big way."

I pull him closer. "I'll show you how I feel."

We lock lips again, but this time I kiss him like a savage, with total abandon and a deep aching hunger. I meant everything I said, and a lot more besides that I left unspoken. I've never met anyone who made me yearn for them before. Sex has always been strictly a physical act for me, but with Aiden there are emotions in play too. I *need* to join with him. I want to arouse the same feelings in him that I'm experiencing. I want him to want me the same way I want him. I want him to *ache* to have me inside him. These feelings are all new to me. I've never cared what the other person felt before.

I pull back from the kiss, my breathing jagged, my dick bloated with need. "Go fetch the supplies," I whisper against his lips.

"Where are they?"

"Bedside table."

He hops off my lap and disappears into the bedroom, returning soon after, stark naked and sporting a proud stiffy that reaches almost to his belly button. I lock my fingers around the back of my head and lean back, feasting on the view. He takes his time walking back to me, a seductive smile on his lips. He may have an impressive length, but it's skinny enough that it doesn't look out of place on his slim frame. His body is lightly toned, firm in all the right places, as you'd expect in one so young when *the body beautiful* is so much easier to achieve. Not like me. I have to work hard to stay in shape.

He tosses the bottle of lube and a handful of condoms on the coffee table, within easy reach, and then climbs back onto my lap, already looking like the cat that got the cream. I drop my hands to my sides, ready to stroke any parts that need stroking. "One of us is overdressed," he purrs, unbuttoning my shirt and pressing kisses along the arc of my pecs, turning my dick into a rod of granite. His other hand deftly unzips my fly and he quickly frees my aching hard-on, causing a gasp to escape my lips. I pull my shirt off and discard it on the floor.

He goes down on me, like he did in the lift, and all my nerve endings light up like a starry night. His tongue licks and flicks around the crown, before gliding down my full length and back up to the top. Then he takes me in his mouth and I'm in heaven once more. I grit my teeth as he opens wide and gorges himself, his head bobbing up and down and cute moany noises resonating in the back of his throat. Using both his hand and mouth to devastating effect, he quickly makes a mockery of any stamina I might have thought I possessed. Way too soon I feel my balls tighten and I groan, knowing I can't take much more of this glorious torture.

"Stand up," I yelp when the sensations become too much to bear. He obeys immediately and I discard the rest of my clothes. Then I wrap my fist around his rigid length, gently massaging it in long strokes as it twitches in my hand like a divining rod. I switch to using my mouth and he rests his hands on my shoulders as he softly moans and quivers. I can only take about half of his length before my gag reflex tries to kick in, but already I can taste the salty-sweetness of his juices starting to flow. I take care not to push him over the brink, pulling away the moment he starts whimpering in earnest.

He lubes himself up as I roll on a condom and then he climbs back onto my lap. He looks me in the eyes as he very gingerly eases himself down onto me, taking his time, making gentle rhythmic movements, until he finally has me fully seated inside. And then he just sits there in my lap, gazing at me, a sexy smirk beaming across his face.

"I feel so in charge being on top," he tells me.

I give him a good-natured grunt. "It's just an illusion. I could flip you on your back and soon have you begging for mercy."

"I'd divorce you tomorrow. Now, tell me you love me and if I'm not totally convinced I'm going to squeeze my muscles so tight it'll shatter every bone in your dick."

"There aren't any bones in my dick."

"Say it," Aiden insists.

"I love you. Happy?"

"Not in the slightest. Do you love me or not?"

"Yes. I love you. Now get your arse moving."

230

"Say it like you mean it."

I look him deep in the eyes. "I love you so much I'd chop off my own balls and eat them for breakfast if my dick so much as winked at anyone else."

Aiden giggles. "That's more like it."

He lifts up onto his haunches and begins a slow bouncing action, gradually working up speed until his thigh muscles are getting a good workout. I bite my lip, revelling in the tight heat of his arse. Despite the thickness of my girth, he milks me magnificently, his rigorous gliding action courtesy of copious amounts of lube. I gasp as I can feel the tsunami already threatening to rip through me. I can't believe how my stamina has completely deserted me on this of all nights. It's embarrassing.

"No. No," I groan out loud at the excruciating agony of trying to fight my orgasm.

"You want me to stop?"

"Hell no! Keep doing what you're doing." As I reply to Aiden, my traitorous body takes advantage of my momentary lapse in concentration, releasing a fresh batch of sex hormones into my bloodstream—the type that tip you over the edge. The only thing I can do now is chase my orgasm. I stop fighting it and instead embrace it to the hilt, attempting to get mind, body and spirit to converge at the exact point of release. That's how you achieve the best orgasms; when your whole being is totally in sync.

"Oh fuck!" I mutter, all my muscles tightening as my body prepares itself.

Aiden recognises I'm close and raises his

tempo to another level, his flailing hard-on slapping against my torso, begging for my attention. I wrap my fist around it and pump it hard, matching Aiden's own tempo. "Shit!" he groans. Moments later he releases his load, the sight of which sends me over the edge too. I let out a shuddering growl as a wave of euphoria washes over me and I fight to hang onto it as long as I can, trying not to tumble off the crest too early before it naturally dissipates.

Finally we're both fully spent and Aiden lifts off me and rolls off the sofa onto the floor. He lies supine, his chest heaving. I remove the condom, tying a knot in it, and then I slide down onto the floor and use my shirt to wipe Aiden's sticky outpouring off my torso.

I lie down beside him and we gaze up at the ceiling together, in silent recovery mode, until our pulses slowly return to something resembling normality.

"I always knew you were going to be a good fuck and you certainly didn't disappoint."

"Did we just fuck?" Aiden asks, his tone full of mischief. "I couldn't tell, it was over so quickly."

"Cheeky little runt! What did you expect when you've been playing hard to get since the moment we met? It creates heightened tension."

"You said you were going to fuck my brains out, but I'm pleased to report they're still intact."

I twist my head to gaze at him. "Seriously, though, how was it for you?"

He holds out his right hand, palm down, and waggles it from side to side. The hand gesture for *so-so.*

"Oh that's bloody charming! Our wedding night

and you tell me it was *meh*."

"I'm joking. Although to be honest, in general, I'm not a big fan of anal. Blowjobs are more my thing."

"And you wait until we're married to tell me this?"

"I enjoyed it tonight. It's like birthday cake. You have to save it for a special occasion, otherwise it's just cake."

"Oh, you think we're only having it once a year?"

Aiden shrugs. "I've not had a lot of experience in these matters and I've sometimes found it painful in the past. Maybe I've been doing it wrong, though. It's getting easier each time, especially since I discovered the importance of lube. A-spit-and-a-prayer doesn't work for me. That's why I made sure I was well lubricated tonight."

"Not a fan of anal," I mutter to myself, finding it hard to believe that Aiden waited until this precise moment to tell me.

Aiden chuckles. "Maybe you should have asked what my favourite motto is before you married me."

"Oh God! I'm almost afraid to ask now. Go on. What is it?"

"Better out than in."

"Well, Aiden Foxwell-Oden, it's going to be my mission to persuade you otherwise." We switch back to gazing at the ceiling until I remember there's another point I wish to make. "And don't go expecting me to say I love you every time we do it. I've told you once and you don't need telling again."

Aiden unexpectedly reaches out and takes my hand, squeezing it gently. "I won't need reminding. How could I forget? It's the nicest thing you've ever said to me and a big step up from when you offered to rearrange my features."

"Yes, well, you do like to push your luck sometimes, but I'm glad it didn't come to that. It would have been a shame. I quite like your features the way they are."

"Don't say nice things about me, Mackenzie. It makes me nervous."

"Why?"

"Because I'm certain you're going to take it away in the next sentence."

"Obviously you're lacking in self-confidence. I can't blame you for that. You're still trying to digest the fact that we're married. You're probably wondering how you managed to bag such a charming, sophisticated, worldly gentleman as myself."

"You're certainly a catch, Mackenzie. I had no trouble at all snaring you in my trap."

"Shall we just agree to call it a draw and stop this one-upmanship? It would make life so much easier if we agreed to be buddies from now on. How about it, Aid?"

He sits bolt upright and glares at me. "Don't call me Aid. It makes me sound like a benefit concert."

I sit up and face him. "Okay, but could you do me a favour? Now that we're married, do you think you could possibly start calling me Mac? That's what all my friends call me."

"You're my husband, not a cheeseburger. If you want me to shorten your name I'll call you

Ken. That's much classier."

"Don't even think about it."

"What's wrong with Ken? I like Ken."

"If you start calling me Ken, I'll start calling you Barbie."

"Okay, so maybe I'll call you Zee.

"And maybe you won't. Here's a novel idea, Aiden. Seeing as we're married and we purportedly have a certain amount of fondness for each other, how about you play nice for once and call me Mac *simply because I asked you to.* Is that a good enough reason?"

"Don't be ridiculous."

"Okay. I thought not."

40 – AIDEN

Mackenzie and I are seated on the burgundy chesterfield sofa in the drawing room of Foxwell Manor. It's odd being back here. It doesn't feel the same. I don't belong here anymore. I've grown up an awful lot in the short time I've been away and this place represents everything I wanted to leave behind. The haunting memories, the feeling of being powerless and trapped by my own birthright; all that is behind me now. This place has lost its grip on me.

But my dad will always be my dad, even if we don't necessarily see eye-to-eye. I know I've been a handful since mum died, but he should have been there for me more than he was. He's never been very demonstrative with his affections towards me. I think his dad was the same way with him.

Matilda, our cook-housekeeper, greeted us on arrival. She's the lady who runs the house and has a number of junior staff beneath her. She used to report to my mum, but now she has carte blanche to run things as she sees fit, apart from the security aspect, which is Frankie's domain. Matilda informed us that my dad was on the phone arranging a shoot and would be with us shortly. In the old days, my grandad used to arrange pheasant and partridge shoots in the grounds. Nowadays, Dad has his friends over for clay-pigeon weekends, but I'm sure he could phone them back another time to make the arrangements. He knew what time we were due to arrive.

We only got in from Vegas yesterday and then stayed in London last night before making the journey here by train and taxi. My car is still in Camber Sands with the paintings locked in the boot. The hotel kindly allowed me to leave it there when we told them we were "popping over to Vegas" to get married. They'll be expecting me to move it soon though, so we'll have to head back down to the south coast when we're done here.

I glance over at Mackenzie. He's shuffled further along the sofa so there's a respectable distance between us. I suppose it's a wise precaution, seeing as my dad doesn't know our current status yet and he's probably had enough shocks lately that one more might tip him over the edge. We're still waiting for him to surface. I think he's deliberately letting us stew for a while before he shows his face. Mackenzie sighs heavily and I roll my eyes to demonstrate I agree with the sentiment. I hate to be kept waiting. I never noticed before how deathly silent this house is. The only background noise is the solemn tick of the oak grandfather clock in the hallway. It sounds like a ticking time bomb, counting down the minutes until my dad explodes into the room, a shotgun in his hand, ready to plug me and Mackenzie full of holes. That's probably what he's doing on the phone, arranging his alibi, thinking he can blame it on an accident at the shoot.

"Sorry to keep you both waiting," I hear my dad say over my shoulder, plucking me out of my doom-laden musings.

Mackenzie and I both jump to our feet.

"Sit," my dad insists, while at the same time remaining standing himself.

Lucy—one of our housemaids—arrives with tea. After she's clattered around, serving us all with a cup, the room falls silent once more.

I clear my throat. "Where's Hannah?" I ask tentatively.

"I sent her into town shopping," Dad replies. "I didn't want her involved in any of this." I'm relieved to note his voice is calm and measured. I was expecting him to have jumped down my throat by now. "So, where have you two just come from?"

We answer almost simultaneously, Mackenzie jumping in slightly ahead of me.

"Vegas." "Germany."

We look at each other.

I wasn't planning on mentioning Vegas this early in the conversation, but I guess it's out there now. I turn back to my dad. "Well, Vegas via France and Germany."

Dad scowls. "Vegas? Do you mean Vienna?"

"No. Las Vegas, Nevada," Mackenzie replies.

"That's a hell of a detour on a road trip of Europe, isn't it?"

"Dad, we're married," I blurt out before I can stop myself. I don't know why it just came out like that, but I spent the whole train journey fretting over how I was going to tell him, so I suppose I just had to unburden myself and get it over with.

I hear Mackenzie gasp beside me and watch as my dad turns a ghostly white before stumbling backwards into his favourite armchair. Once again silence reigns, with only the ticking clock to mask the sound of the proverbial pin dropping.

My dad finally says something.

"Do you know, Aiden, most kids satisfy themselves with throwing a wild party when they've got the house to themselves. But not you. Oh no. *You* have to steal the bloody paintings off the wall and then elope to Vegas. Why do you always have to push everything to the limits? I don't know where I went wrong with you. I've been too lenient by far, haven't I? My father would have flailed me alive the moment I stepped in the bloody door."

"Yeah, well, we don't live in the dark ages anymore," I scoff.

Dad wags his finger at me. "Less of your lip, young man."

"Do you want me to hold him down for you, Lord Foxwell?" Mackenzie offers unhelpfully.

I throw him a look. "That's not even funny, Mackenzie. Stay out of this, will you?"

Dad turns on Mackenzie now. "This is all your fault. You're a bad influence. Maybe it's *you* who should be flailed alive."

"Me?" Mackenzie says as if he's innocence personified. "Your son is a lot smarter than either of us, Lord Foxwell. Nobody influences him."

Dad grunts. "Is that so? Well, I suppose you can't keep calling me Lord Foxwell now that you're my son-in-law, so you'd better call me Lotty."

"Lotty?" Mackenzie repeats hesitantly.

"Lancelot," I explain.

"That's…unusual," Mackenzie notes, which only serves to invite my dad to go off on one of his long family history lessons by way of explanation. I roll my eyes as soon as the words start to spill from his mouth, having heard it all before.

"My mother, Lady Amelia, was a remarkable woman. She was voted most beautiful debutante at her coming-out ball, but her looks aside, she was, quite frankly, barking mad. Oh yes, poor old mother liked to hang out with the fairies. She would chat with them in the garden and serve them tea and biscuits, and couldn't understand why little Lotty couldn't see them. I blame it on centuries of inbreeding in the nobility, not to mention her love of the gin bottle. I imagine she had the font water replaced with gin so she could carry on imbibing while I was being christened. Lancelot Festival Herringay were the forenames she allotted me. My father was a reserved man. He was quite strict with me, but he didn't care for confrontation with my mother, preferring instead to let her have her own way in all things. I think he found her utterly bewildering and was at a loss how to handle her. He married her for her looks but got a whole lot more than he bargained for. Fortunately, myself and Aiden take after my father's side of the family. He was a distinguished mathematician and a highly-regarded FRS in his day."

"FRS?" Mackenzie enquires.

"Fellow of the Royal Society," I explain.

"However," Dad continues, "Aiden has shown little sign of putting the brains he inherited to any constructive use. Instead, he takes his

241

amusement in trying to outwit me at every opportunity, sneaking out of the house for his secret trysts, believing I'm unaware of what goes on behind my back. Since my wife passed, I've struggled to fill the gap she left in Aiden's life and, to be honest, I believe he resented me even trying. So I decided it was better to take a backseat and let him come to terms with it in his own time. Maybe that was a mistake. I think he then switched to resenting me for backing away. Our relationship is probably best described as problematic, but he's my son, and no matter what he does he will *always* be my son. All I've ever wanted is for him to be happy. I never expected him to be anything other than himself in private, but the way he presents himself in public is a different matter. He has the family reputation to uphold and I had hoped he would wish to continue the family line and give me a grandchild. And maybe he could have made a go of it with Lady Montgomery's daughter if you hadn't outbid her at the auction, but I suppose now we'll never know."

I step in before Mackenzie and Dad get to locking horns over who did what at the auction. "Look, Dad, I know I'm a disappointment to you, but if you really want me to be happy then you have to give us your blessing. Mackenzie's a good man. He'll grow on you, I promise. I know mum would have been happy for us."

"Aiden, I'm not disappointed in *you*, I'm disappointed in *myself* for not knowing how to be a good father to you. Of course I want you to be happy. I never had a problem with you being gay. Do you remember your Great-Uncle George? He was gay and I was very fond of him. The only real

242

issue I had was that I wanted you to produce an heir so the bloodline doesn't end here. Anyway, you, um,"—my dad suddenly starts stuttering and his cheeks turn beet red—"you don't need to worry about that anymore."

"Why?" I ask, scowling at him, wondering why the sudden change in demeanour. "What do you mean?"

"I have news of my own, Aiden," Dad says sheepishly. "Hannah and I are to be married and since she's keen to have a sprog, it would seem you're off the hook."

My heart leaps into my throat and I have to swallow it back down. "Oh wow! I'm going to have a sibling?"

"You don't mind?" my dad asks tentatively.

"Are you kidding? You could have given me one ten years ago though, that would have been more helpful, but no, of course I don't mind. Congratulations! That's great, Dad."

"Well, let's not jump the gun. We have to get married first. You don't mind having a new mother?"

I feel a sharp twist in my gut and I throw my dad a look. "My mother is dead. No-one can replace her. Hannah will be your wife. She will never be my mother."

Dad holds his hands up, trying to stop my rant. "Yes, okay, Aiden. That's fine. Poor choice of words. I simply was asking if you mind me taking a new wife."

"No, of course not. I really like Hannah. She's good for you. I was sort of hoping you'd realise that one day and not let her slip through your fingers."

"So we're good?"

I nod. "Yeah, but who's to say me and Mackenzie won't have kids, anyway?"

Dad chuckles. "Has no-one ever explained the mechanics of a lady to you, Aiden? They're the ones that have the baby-making equipment."

I roll my eyes. "Don't be silly, Dad. I meant using a surrogate."

"Well, that would be marvellous, Aiden."

"Wait a minute," Mackenzie says, turning to me. "Don't you think you and I should discuss these sorts of things first, in private, before you start making announcements to the world?"

"I wasn't announcing anything. I was simply pointing out that I'm still perfectly capable of continuing the family line."

"Really?" Mackenzie says. "And who says *you'd* be the sperm donor if we decide to have a kid?"

"Because I'm the obvious choice."

"Do you want to explain that to me," Mackenzie says, sounding annoyed by my presumption.

"Well, for a start, I'm the one with the good breeding."

"And what do you know of my heritage?" he asks.

"You're a thief, Mackenzie. It's in your blood."

"It's a profession, Aiden, not a faulty gene."

"Aside from that, we'd also want our kid to be smart—I don't think I need expand on that—and then there's your age to consider."

"My age! I'm thirty-three. I'm still in my bloody prime."

"But we wouldn't have one straight away. We'd

want to be settled in our new life first and then we'd have to find the right surrogate. It could be another five years before we're parents, so clearly I am the only logical choice for the sperm donor. Let's face it, if you want some drinking water, you go to the spring, not the stagnant pond."

"Well you didn't think it was stagnant when you were lapping it up and telling me it tasted like salted caramel."

I gasp. "That's too much information in front of my dad, Mackenzie."

"Look," my dad says, "would you two mind arguing in your own time. We do have other important matters we need to discuss, as I'm sure you're aware."

Mackenzie and I immediately fall silent. *Oh shit! Here we go!*

We need to talk about the fact there's a photograph in the frame where my painting is meant to be. Not just *any* painting. My most expensive painting, Aiden."

"You spotted that a lot sooner than I thought," I reply shamefaced.

"Lucy spotted it when she gave it a flick with the feather duster. Apparently it wafted. Paintings don't tend to waft. She called Frankie up to take a look and there were two obvious giveaways. The white strip at the bottom that said *Printed by Quickie Prints*."

I cringe. "Oh, did I forget to cut that off?"

"And the fact it was Blu-Tacked to the frame."

"I was in a hurry."

Mackenzie grunts. "What a fantastic inside man you turned out to be."

Dad glances from me to Mackenzie. "So I take it you two were in this together."

"It was his idea," Mackenzie says, pointing a finger at me.

I gasp. "No, it was *your* idea, I just gave you the opportunity and the means."

"You conned me into doing it. You know you did," he argues.

"How could my son con a grown man into stealing something?" my dad says to Mackenzie.

"Yeah, explain that," I say, rounding on Mackenzie.

"You didn't just con me into stealing a painting, you then grassed me up to the police too."

"That was because I needed to teach you a lesson, and at least I was willing to share the spoils with you. You were going to run off and keep them all to yourself."

"What you mean is you needed someone to cash the painting in for you, so you blackmailed me with that security camera footage."

I narrow my eyes at him. "Are we really going to do this in front of my dad?"

I hear my dad chuckling to himself. "Well, Mackenzie, you've certainly got your hands full. Now you know what I felt like at times. But let me tell you this. You've made your bed and you'd damn well better lie in it, or you'll have me to answer to."

I give Mackenzie a smug look. "Yeah, you're stuck with me now."

Mackenzie rolls his eyes. "God help me!"

I turn back to my dad. "Look, about the

painting. I know what I did was a very bad thing, but it would have been mine in a few years' time anyway."

"A few years!" Dad scoffs. "I'm not planning on kicking the bucket for at least another forty years."

"Yes, well, maybe that's the point. It would be no use to me then. I needed a down payment on my inheritance. Me and Mackenzie need to start a new life together and you wouldn't want me living in poverty, now would you?"

"Yeah, all the rich families pass on part of their inheritance early for tax avoidance purposes," Mackenzie adds.

Dad huffs. "What would you know about paying your bloody taxes? You're a thief."

"*Was* a thief," Mackenzie points out. "That lifestyle is behind me now."

"Lifestyle! Don't glam it up. You're a rogue of the first order."

"Yes he is," I agree. "That's what first attracted me to him. That and the dimple in his chin."

"You mean the bulge in my pants," Mackenzie mutters under his breath.

I throw him a look.

"Truth be told, Aiden, you actually did me a favour," Dad says.

"What? How do you work that out?" I ask, turning my attention back to Dad.

"Ever since I bought the bloody thing I've been fretting about just such a thing happening. It's turned into a liability. I deeply regret my impetuous decision to buy it and if you can turn it back into cash I'll happily split the proceeds with you. Let's say an equal fifty-fifty split. That way you'll have enough to buy yourself a decent house and settle down in the style to which you're accustomed. Think of it as a sort of wedding dowry."

I glance at Mackenzie. He shrugs his shoulders resignedly.

"Thanks, Dad. We accept your offer of a dowry. Mackenzie will arrange to sell the painting as soon as we get back to London."

41 – MACKENZIE

Being back in England is like slamming headfirst into reality after our surreal trip to Vegas. That trip to Foxwell Manor certainly brought us back to Earth with a thud and then we had to go straight back to Camber Sands to pick Aiden's car up. It's been a crazy week.

For the time being, Aiden has moved into my London flat with me. We've rented an undercover parking space to store Aiden's car, and the paintings are hidden under a pile of blankets in the wardrobe in my spare bedroom, for want of a better place to stash them.

I'm dreading phoning Lenny and asking him to believe I really do have the genuine painting this time. He was pretty pissed off with me when the last one turned out to be a fake. Maybe I'll phone him tomorrow.

Aiden is oddly quiet as we sit around the kitchen table having breakfast. I can't help wondering what's going on in that devious brain of his, so I decide to give it a prod and see what spills out.

"Do you get the feeling we've been conned into giving your father half of the proceeds from the painting we stole?"

"Well, it did belong to him in the first place," Aiden points out.

"I'm feeling quite sick about this whole thing now I've had a chance to mull it over. I was supposed to be getting £10 million for this job.

Then it was halved because you and I were going to split it, and now your father's getting half, and you and I are only getting £2.5 million each. What can you buy for that sort of money these days?"

"A beach house at Camber Sands?" Aiden suggests with a cheesy grin.

"We'll have to hope Lenny can be persuaded the painting is genuine this time."

"Well, maybe you don't need to worry about that anymore."

"Why? What do you mean?"

"I've been thinking things through and I've come to a decision."

"What's that?"

"I've decided not to sell."

"Not to sell! What are you talking about?"

"Don't you see? This is lunacy. We already have everything we need and we're about to jeopardise all that for what? *More* of everything? We're not a pair of mercenaries. Look, this is just a game that got out of hand. I was bored. I needed something to occupy my mind and bring a touch of glamour and excitement into my life. It ended up better than I could have ever hoped for and I hope you feel the same way too. You came to steal a painting and instead you stole my heart. I'd swap a painting for love any day. I think we should be grateful and stick with what we have and not push it any further. Why risk what we have? Why risk *us*? Why risk our freedom? This is the first time in my adult life that I've been happy and I don't want to jeopardise that."

My stomach flips and I feel the burn of nausea

behind my sternum. "So what exactly is it that you're proposing?"

"I think we should give the Raphael back."

"Give it back?" I can't believe what I'm hearing. The boy's lost his marbles. "Your father doesn't want it back. He said as much."

"Not to him. I'm talking about giving it back to the people."

"What people?"

"Society. We need to give the painting back to the public."

"Have you gone insane?"

"Think about it, Mackenzie. There's no greater accomplishment that you and I could ever hope to achieve in our lifetimes than to give back to the world a missing masterpiece."

"As opposed to being filthy rich," I remind him.

"You were just complaining that £5 million between us wasn't enough."

"It's a whole lot better than nothing."

"We *have* to give it back."

"No we don't."

"It's not your decision to make. The fake is the one you stole, remember. I took the real one. It's mine. You can keep a hundred-percent of the proceeds from the fake, but we have to give up the real one. It doesn't belong on the wall of a private residence. It belongs to the world."

"Unlike you, Aiden, my mind is unsullied by feelings of guilt or compassion for my fellow man. I have no compunction in continuing to deprive the world of the Raphael."

"But I don't want to always be looking over my

shoulder and wondering when my past is going to catch up with me. I've made up my mind, Mackenzie, and you're either with me or against me. So which is it?"

"I'm mulling over my options," I tell him in a haughty tone.

He scowls at me. "What options?"

"Well, I suppose I could shoot you and then I'd have both of the paintings to myself."

"Except you don't have a gun, right?" Aiden says tentatively.

I look him right in the eyes. "Who says I don't have a gun?"

"You're an art thief, not an armed robber."

"Maybe I have a sports rifle."

He smirks at me. "You're not the wax-jacket-and-wellies type."

This is true, nevertheless his smug look incites me to persevere. "I could stab you with a kitchen knife."

"I'd bleed all over your Axminster carpet. Forensics would have a field day."

"I could strangle you with my bare hands. It wouldn't be the first time I've been tempted."

"And during the ensuing struggle I'd scratch your eyes out, leaving lots of telltale DNA under my nails."

"Hmm…might be worth it," I mumble, unimpressed by Aiden's counterthreats, "just to see the look on your face as my grip tightens."

"So you're not willing to accept my decision?"

"The point I was trying to make is that I *could* kill you, but then I'd be left with a dead husband. Dead husbands don't tend to be very good in bed and since we're only at the start of our sexual exploration phase, I'd rather like to keep you alive, for the time being at least."

"Then I'd better make sure I hold something back, so you don't get bored with me too quickly."

"My other option, as your husband, would be to tie you to the bedpost and whip some sense into you." I pause as I let that image linger in my mind awhile. "Actually, that option has definite merit."

Aiden rolls his eyes. "Enough of your kinky fantasies, Mackenzie, we're supposed to be having a serious discussion. How long have you been in this art theft game?"

"All my life."

"So unless you're very bad at it you must already be a wealthy man."

"I have enough to retire on."

"So what's your problem?"

I grunt. "I'll tell you what my problem is. I'm greedy. Enough isn't enough. I want *more* than enough. A lot more. More than I know what to do with."

"I'll go out to work if it'll help."

I snort out a laugh. "You? Work?"

"Don't say it like that. You're the one who put the suggestion in my head when we first met. You told me I should go out and get a job."

"Do you even know what a CV is?"

He shrugs. "It's some sort of venereal disease, isn't it? What's that got to do with anything?"

"I rest my case."

"Come on, Mackenzie. You know it's the right thing to do. This isn't just any painting. This is an important piece of history. We have to give it back."

"Don't you think your father will have something to say about that?"

"I'll handle my dad. I just want to know if you're on board with it or not."

"Why do you have to be such a flaky little shit?"

"I like to keep you on your toes."

"And how do you propose we give it back without getting ourselves arrested for being in possession of stolen property?"

"It was stolen decades ago in a different country. How could we be held responsible for that crime?"

"They'd still want to know how we got hold of it. Black market trades are illegal, in case you hadn't guessed."

"We could just post it to the National Gallery."

"Post it?" I scoff. "What do you mean, wrap it up in brown paper and slip it in the mailbox?"

"Don't be ridiculous. We'd have to send it by a trackable service."

"Oh, you mean like Special Delivery," I jeer in an incredulous voice. "Because don't forget, we'd get a whole £500 insurance cover with that. After all, you never know when something of value might go missing in the post."

"I'm sure we could purchase additional cover."

"What, for £10 million?"

Aiden sighs. "Okay, if you don't like that idea we'll hire a van and deliver it ourselves."

I rub my brow where my exasperation with Aiden is threatening to bring on a migraine. "If we hire a van they'll be able to trace the number plates back to which hire shop we used and they'll have CCTV footage of us, not to mention credit card records."

"We could pay cash."

"They'd still need to take details off my driving licence."

"So why don't you break into the museum, hang it on the wall, and no-one would be any the wiser?"

"You don't think anyone would notice this sudden addition to their collection?"

Aiden shrugs. "Doesn't matter. It's not a crime to donate a painting."

I screw my nose up in what I hope is a good impression of utter contempt. "I'm not going to break into the National Gallery to *add* a painting to their collection. What kind of thief do you think I am?"

Aiden is undeterred and continues with the relentless flow of idiotic suggestions. "Okay, then we'll deliver it to them by hand. We don't need to hire a van we can carry it there on the Tube."

"We? You mean *me*, don't you?"

"Well, you're a better liar than me."

I laugh so hard I almost swallow my tonsils.

Aiden sighs. "Look, I'll come with you if you like. At least as far as the door. How's that?"

"So you want me to knock on the door of the National Gallery and say 'Hi! Here's a stolen masterpiece I found earlier.' Is that your plan?"

"You wouldn't have to say anything. You're

255

supposed to be a random courier delivering a random package. You'd have no idea what's in it."

"I think the shape sort of gives it away."

"Okay, so an anonymous donor left it to the museum in his will. Probably happens all the time. All we need to do is get you kitted out so you look like a courier and no-one will question you. I'm sure we must be able to find a workman's jacket and trousers in a charity shop."

"Good," I snap. "I'm sure you'll look very fetching in them."

"Get real, Mackenzie. Can you honestly see me in polyester? The job is yours."

"Say I agree to go through with this lunatic scheme of yours, what about the CCTV cameras? Have you thought about those?"

"If you wear a baseball cap and keep your head down, you'll be fine. That's how they do it in the movies."

"Seriously, Aiden, there's a lot of déjà vu going through my head right now."

"What do you mean?"

"I'm starting to feel like a first-class idiot. The way I did when I woke up in a skip after you drugged me. You know, right before you called the police on me. This isn't some sort of double-cross, is it? I'm not going to find the police waiting for me when I get to the museum, am I?"

"Mackenzie!" he gasps. "How could you even think such a thing? We're married now. Did we not vow to stand by each other, come what may? Besides, you know I can't testify against my husband."

"No, but your father could testify. Suppose he had the room bugged when we went back to Foxwell Manor?"

"Like you said, Mackenzie, he can't involve the police for his own reasons. Stop being paranoid. Trust me. We can do this."

I groan, defeated. "I hate you, Aiden."

"No you don't!" Aiden throws himself at me, wrapping his arms around my neck and kissing my face. "Thank you. You don't know how much this means to me. Now I know I mean more to you than that stupid painting."

I lean back to look him in the eyes. "You realise how awful this is going to look on my résumé?"

"You're retired now, Mackenzie. Remember?"

"Oh really! It doesn't feel like it."

"There are just some loose ends to wrap up, that's all."

"So when does this retirement actually begin?"

"As soon as we've set the world to rights," he says with a jubilant smile.

42 – AIDEN

I'm so happy. I feel like my life is finally on track. This morning Mackenzie and I paid a visit to an estate agent in Islington and put Mackenzie's flat on the market. And when he finds a buyer, we're going to put the proceeds towards buying my dream home in Camber Sands. I feel so blessed right now.

We had a long chat last night in bed and we're agreed that the most important thing that came out of this whole episode is that we ended up together. And to prove he really is on board with my plan, Mackenzie said that if I want my conscience clear, we have to give back *both* paintings—the copy as well as the original. I can't argue with his logic. That seventeenth-century copy was also stolen from a museum and I'm sure they'd be extremely happy to have it back, even if the original has resurfaced.

I've spoken to my dad about giving the painting back and the conversation went so much better than I could have hoped. I told him the way I feel and he came clean about how he plans to rewrite his will once he and Hannah have a child. He said I have made it abundantly clear that I have no interest in the ancestral home and it's important to him that Foxwell Manor is kept in the family for future generations. Therefore, his and Hannah's child—or eldest child, if they have more than one—will be named heir to Foxwell Manor and all its contents. Dad said that he *had* intended for his fifty-percent share of the proceeds from the Raphael to go into a bank account with my name on it. It was to be the balance of my inheritance, as I wasn't getting a share in the house. I told him I'm really not worried about any inheritance, just so long as I get to keep my car.

So that was that. The bottom line is my dad just wants me to be happy, but also for Foxwell Manor to stay in the family, and so this new arrangement suits us both. As for me, I can't wait for this whole episode to be behind us so that Mackenzie and I can get on with the rest of our lives.

It's weird but since I've left home I'm on better terms with my dad than perhaps I've ever been. One thing I know for sure is that Hannah is good for him. He's mellowed an awful lot since they got together. She keeps him young and active and fit. She's his squash partner, his golf partner, his travel companion and his friend. I'm happy for them both and glad they're getting married. Dad's already asked me to be best man and Mackenzie to be an usher. It's starting to feel like I'm part of a proper family unit again.

Aiden and I take the fifteen-minute journey by Tube from Islington to Trafalgar Square, each with a precious work of art under one arm. Aiden is carrying the copy and I have the original, all wrapped up in brown paper and addressed to The Curator of the National Gallery. We're both wearing gloves and we've got our baseball caps pulled down low over our eyes. I'm kitted out in an approximation of a courier's outfit. In the end I went for a navy cotton-twill jacket and matching trousers.

Trafalgar Square is busy with the usual amount of tourists for a mild autumn day with watery sunshine seeping through the thinning cloud cover. We hurry past the hordes, gaining a bit of unwanted attention on account of the conspicuous packages under our arms. Heading around the back of the gallery, we arrive on Orange Street, where the delivery entrance is located. Aiden hands me the other painting.

"Good luck!" he says.

I huff. "Knowing how flaky you are, let me say this. If you should change your mind again at some point in the future and decide you want the Raphael back, please find someone else to steal it for you."

Aiden laughs. "Don't worry. This is it. Never again. We're agreed about that, right?"

"I'm not in the habit of stealing things only to give them back."

"Trust me. A whole weight is going to be lifted off our shoulders when you do this," he assures me.

"The only difference I'm going to notice is the gaping hole in my bank balance."

Aiden plants a kiss on my lips. "You're my hero, Mackenzie, and that's priceless."

I roll my eyes. "You'd better go before someone spots us loitering suspiciously."

"Okay. I'll see you back at the flat."

I watch Aiden go. We have two bags packed at the flat, ready for a quick getaway, should things go drastically wrong. As soon as he disappears around the corner I make my move. I enter the building through the grey *Inward Goods* door. My heart is thumping harder than when I'm actually *stealing* artwork. I don't usually turn up in broad daylight with the stolen goods tucked under my arm. I walk down a short corridor to a door on the right that's slightly ajar. I peek through the gap and I can see a uniformed middle-aged gent sat behind a desk, staring at a computer screen. I take a deep breath and then tap lightly on the door. He looks up.

"Can I help?"

I push the door open and as I enter I note the badge sewn onto the chest pocket of the man's jacket. It says *National Gallery* and beneath that *Henry.*

"I have a delivery for the curator," I say in a clear, confident tone, belying my jangling nerves. "Two in fact."

Henry taps his keyboard and scowls at his screen. "I have no record of any incoming deposits today. Where did this consignment originate?"

I gulp. "Oh, well, no, there won't be any record. It was sudden. An old lady died and left you these in her will." My hands are starting to sweat all over the brown paper packaging. "Do you mind if I just pop these down here. They're quite heavy." I set the paintings down, leaning them against the wall and rub my hands on my trousers.

"And who is this old lady?"

"I wouldn't know. I'm just the courier."

"Well, whose name is on the order?"

"Oh...er...Mrs...Nadal."

"And how do you know these paintings were left to us in a will if you're just the courier?"

"She happened to mention it when I went to collect them. She said she wanted to donate them to the nation."

He arches his brow at me. "Oh, you spoke to her. The dead lady."

"Yes. I mean before she died, obviously."

"So she phoned to book a courier to implement a clause in her will before she'd even died."

"That's correct. Apparently she liked to plan ahead. She told me to be sure to get a signature."

"She said this with her dying breath, did she?"

"More or less," I reply sheepishly, knowing full well he doesn't believe a single word of my pathetic story and I can't say I blame him. I'm terrible at making things up on the spot and this whole scenario is way out of my comfort zone. I'm itching to make a run for it.

He picks up his phone. "Just wait there a moment, please," he says in a stern voice that I know spells trouble.

I decide it's time to split. I'm not hanging around for him to call security. I bolt out of there, with him calling after me, telling me to wait, but I manage to make it back onto the street before the security people turn up. Retracing my route up Orange Street and back across Trafalgar Square, I quickly reach the Charing Cross Tube station, where I duck into the toilets and ditch the baseball cap, jacket and trousers. I have a second pair of thin trousers on underneath in readiness and I pop on a pair of black-rimmed glasses to complete the transformation. If they try to track me on CCTV, hopefully I won't be recognisable as the same man who entered the toilets and they'll lose the trail.

I head on back to my flat, where Aiden is waiting. This whole episode feels so bizarre. What kind of thief hands a painting back? I never thought anyone could make an honest man of me—neither by means of marriage or like this. What is Aiden doing to me?

44 – AIDEN

Tonight is a special celebration. Not only is it my birthday, we're also celebrating the good deed of the century—me and Mackenzie having returned the two paintings to public ownership. They are back on display for anyone to view free of charge and this doesn't just benefit the current populace; they'll be there for all the future generations of art lovers to admire too. The Raphael is already five hundred years old. My family's ownership of it was just a fleeting moment in its long history. It will outlive many more generations of Foxwells after I'm gone, but I know my place in history now. Mackenzie and I have made a difference. When we get old and look back over our lives, even if we never again do anything else worthwhile, we can still be satisfied that our lives had meaning and purpose. Maybe that's why the fates brought me and Mackenzie together, so we could do this amazing thing. To right a wrong that occurred in another era, in war-torn Europe, and return Raphael's self-portrait to a place where it can be appreciated by all.

It makes me glow inside to know we both carried through with such a noble gesture. I'm especially proud of Mackenzie. This whole episode has changed him. *I've* changed him. I'm certain the old Mackenzie never would have given up the painting. As much as he jokes about wanting to kill me half the time, I know this really must be love. He could have taken the painting from me at any time and I would have been helpless to stop him. But he didn't. Because I'm worth more to him than any painting; even one as precious as the Raphael. Money can't buy you companionship and when you're as difficult to please as we both are, you can't afford to let go when you find the one who's right for you. And he's definitely the one for me. He's the only one to make my heart beat faster just by being in the same room.

Mackenzie booked a table for my birthday at one of the restaurants at the top of The Shard. The view is mind-blowing—floor-to-ceiling windows that provide a 40-mile panorama of the city and beyond. It's especially magical in the evening with everything lit up. The surrounding skyscrapers thrust up from the earth like glistening ice stalagmites.

We both enjoyed a delicious steak for our main course and I'm just perusing the dessert menu when I notice in my peripheral vision that there's an ensemble of waiters and waitresses around our table. I look up to see one of them is holding a cake with lit candles and then Mackenzie sets them off singing Happy Birthday. All the other diners in the restaurant fall silent and everyone gawks in our direction. It's the most embarrassing moment of my entire life. I don't know where to look. My cheeks are on fire and knowing that everyone can see how embarrassed I am makes it even more excruciating. I know I'm supposed to find this touching but I'm just praying for it to be over. Thankfully it soon is. The cake is placed on the table, alongside a bunch of pink and yellow roses. I mumble my appreciation to them all and then Mackenzie and

I are alone once more.

I untie the gift card from the roses so I can read it.

To my inside man,

It was the best of times and the worst of times, but I wouldn't change anything about these last three months because look where we ended up. It's been a rollercoaster journey and I've no idea what we're going to do next year to top this year's experiences. Happy birthday!

The L-word.

M

He literally wrote *The L-word*.

I smirk at him. "The L-word?"

"I told you in Vegas that I've said it once and you don't need to hear it again."

"Oh but I do," I insist. "It's my birthday."

He gets up and comes around the table to give me a kiss. "I love you," he whispers against my lips as he pulls away. He retakes his seat and then I notice the gift box he left on the table in front of me.

"What's this?"

"Open it."

I lift the lid and my heart skips a beat. Nestled on a velvet cushion inside the box is the tellin shell I gave Mackenzie on the night of the theft. Mackenzie has had it set in a gold mount and attached to a pendant.

"It's back with its rightful owner now," he tells

me.

I couldn't even think of any witty comment to make about him giving me my own gift back. It was just such a beautiful gesture that I welled up.

45 – MACKENZIE

So, the missing masterpiece is no longer missing. It's back on public display, as is the copy. Aiden and I won't even be going down in history as the men who gave those great works of art back to the public, so I guess we'll just have to content ourselves with being a pair of unsung heroes.

I'm still considering writing my autobiography, albeit anonymously. I think it could be a bestseller. I'm probably going to call it *How Not To Thieve* because this is definitely not the way to go about it. I like that title. I think it has a nice ring to it. And I do like a nice ring. A nice tight ring. Aiden has a tight ring. On his left hand. Must be all the wining and dining we've indulged in since we got married. After all, we *are* still in our honeymoon period, and I think after what we've been through together since we met, we're entitled to live it up a little.

I'm not sure how long this honeymoon period will last, but I'm not worried. Once the sheen starts wearing off this shiny new relationship, there's an obvious way to put the sparkle back into it. We could go back into thieving. Between us, we make a red-hot team, and Aiden's going to need *something* to keep that devilishly cunning mind of his occupied. I know he said *never again*, but let's be honest, Aiden just couldn't stomach the idea of having stolen from his own father. That's what was really eating him up inside. I understood how he felt. After all, I married into the family, so it was the same for me. It felt like

I'd shat in my own nest. That's why it made sense that if we were going to donate one back to the public, we donate them both.

Anyway, that's all behind us now and I've started thinking about how nice it would be, not to steal for someone else, but to steal for ourselves, so we can have a nice work of art hung on our *own* wall, in the Camber Sands property.

Truth is, I've got my heart set on a Caravaggio. One in particular. It's called *The Cardsharps.* It's probably my all-time favourite painting. It has a strange history, much like the Raphael. It went missing for almost a hundred years before turning up in a private collection in Zurich. It's now in a museum in Fort Worth, Texas.

Well, *one* version of it is.

You see, Caravaggio painted *three* versions. He was a most unorthodox artist, renowned for working with ordinary people that he'd simply pulled in from the streets to pose for him. He'd skip the traditional route of sketching a rough draft first, instead painting freehand directly onto the canvas, and often producing multiple versions. His unique way of working, including how he shunned natural light in favour of directed lamplight, is what makes his pieces stand out from the rest and why I love his work so much.

There's another version of *The Cardsharps* in a British museum, but it's the third version that appears most accessible. I've recently heard on the grapevine that it's in a private collection in a remote hilltop villa in Umbria in Italy. Sounds like a tempting target. Maybe too tempting to ignore.

So who knows, the next time Aiden decides he's bored and needs something to stimulate his mind, we might be dusting off the DB11 and taking another jaunt across Europe. If I know Aiden, he isn't going to be content with playing at being a "normal" person for very long. I reckon once the thrill of furnishing our new home starts to wear off, he's going to get itchy feet, and I'll be ready and waiting with the perfect solution. He's had a taste of thieving now and it's hard to find anything else in life to match the kind of buzz it can give you. It's addictive. I should know.

I have a feeling the adventure has just begun...

FOLLOW ME & MORE BOOKS

To be notified of new releases you can follow me on Amazon, Goodreads and Bookbub, where you will also find a list of all my other titles. If you enjoyed HOW NOT TO THIEVE and have a moment to leave a brief review on any of those platforms it would be greatly appreciated.

Thank you for choosing my book!

Printed in Poland
by Amazon Fulfillment
Poland Sp. z o.o., Wrocław

56299529R00164